THE SAUCY

JUICY PAIN

GAME

Book One of Two

By Anita Kirk

Dedication

Anita's most popular fan would be her father before he sadly got dementia, and he is now devastatingly blowing in the wind.
Anita's family has supported her one hundred percent with her writing, and she thanks them for the encouragement and you for taking the time out of your day to pick her book up and read it.
If you do enjoy reading this book Anita would really appreciate a good review to show other people that you have enjoyed reading.

Acknowledgments

I would like to thank you for taking the time to pick this book out from the millions of books available out there to read, if you do enjoy reading this book, your review would mean the world to Anita Kirk for her to enjoy reading and sharing this book with others on social media or in person would be most appreciated.

Thank you.

Prologue

Warning.

This is a Steamy but brutal fight to the end for the volunteers/victims from various parts of the world, it is a horrific unpredictable game for adults' eyes only to enjoy, it is set in the central American rain forest with plenty of unpredictable weather and intimate special magical moments to remember.

It will keep you falling off your seat with worry for the eight volunteer contestants that have never met before, they do not realise how much danger they are letting themselves in for to win an enormous amount of money if they can stay alive for six weeks with a limited amount of tools in their transparent rook sacks, food, water and sleep.

The minute the volunteers walk into the jungle with their limited tools to help keep them alive, they have a powerful pain-enhancing needle to bring back every pain that they have ever had in their entire lives back with evengencce with it controlling them all at once in between animals, items, game's challenges, dolls, teddies, and people trying to kill them with plenty of blood spilt.

They will be dirty, stinky, and low on energy with red drones telling them what to do with a dog egg timer ruling their lives and only an orange button, a safe room, and a secret room as a saviour.

Friends that become a couple called Leon and Sharon from Wakefield in the United Kingdom watch the pain game from Sharon's couch with them enjoying each others social and sexual company in between each game cracking jokes to try to lighten the mood, and do they ever go live on the pain game?

There are also two celebrities sitting above the victims in the jungle called Niall Orange and Sophie Ball, they comment on different challenges and activities happening live in front of them, they have only got the volunteers red coats as the tool to identify the players with their names on their backs.

In the pain game, there are haunted houses, snow machines, buttons, darkrooms, bubbles that trap them, mazes, pubs and so much more with them all full of dangers that are included in most of their dangerous challenges.

Do the volunteers help each other or are they only out for themselves?

Do any of the volunteer players survive to win the jackpot to share or do they win alone?

How do the relatives react that are left with their family members dead?

If you dare to dive into this unpredictable pain game, you are one of the brave people to roll the rollercoaster of horrors that awaits the players, you will feel the players pain, struggles and stress along the way.

Chapter Seventy – Pop the balloon.

Chapter Seventy-One – Petrol Smell.

Chapter Seventy-Two – Steamy climax.

Chapter Seventy-Three – Removed clothes.

Chapter Seventy-Nine – Camera off.

Chapter Eighty – Nation Watching.

Chapter One

Obstacles

Old friends Sharon and Leon arranged to meet in the popular Crumbs sandwich shop as their normal routine in Wakefield in the United Kingdom.

They sat down and started to look at the menu, with Sharon speaking to Leon in the Crumbs sandwich shop in the town centre for breakfast. "It is nice to see you again in person, Leon. I am glad that you have got a little bit of time away from your police constable job!"

Leon smiled. "Yes, me too, I think it would be lovely for us to spend some time together!"

Sharon reached her fingers over to Leon's over the table. "I am looking forward to us making plenty of memories for us to talk about in the future!"

Leon brushed his hand over his head. "Yeah, I have saved all of my annual leave up, so that I could have a long stint of time away from work!"

Sharon smiled. "I am happy for you, I am desperate to tell you that I noticed a new game being advertised on a television advertisement this morning that anyone can enter into, it is based in the jungle in Central America!"

Leon's eyes lit up. "That sounds interesting!"

Sharon explained. "The snag is, it isn't a normal natural environment because it has got unpredictable warm weather with it being in January, and there are extra dangers such as a haunted house and a church full of dangerous items!"

Leon rolled his eyes. "January is okay, at least we can snuggle up and watch the pain game cosy and warm together while we snack on junk food and enjoy a few beers!"

Sharon spoke with her hands. "Strangely, there is also a snowstorm machine, mazes for them to get lost in and many more unbelievable crazy situations thrown at the players that will upset the apple cart!"

Leon sounded curious, scratching his head. "So, how did they pick the game players, I wonder?"

Sharon looked down at her phone screen. "It has got plenty of comments on my app called Socials, it is a popular social media site!"

Leon looked at Sharon's Socials. "Yes, people are saying that they like the name the pain game, and it is being talked about well!"

Sharon shrugged her shoulders. "The people in charge of the game will have picked the players at random, or I presume this is true from the people that entered volunteering to play the game to win some money, and I would think that a game would be hard to play in the jungle with it being full of cheetahs!"

Leon giggled slightly, sounding intrigued fidgeting with his hands on the table. "At least it's sunny outside today so, please tell me what it is about this game that makes it more interesting than others on television at the moment, please tell me!"

Sharon played with her hands. "We will find out when we watch it!"

Leon fidgeted. "I am interested to find out, we could watch it together when it is live on television at my house or your house, and I am pleased that you have got some time away from your bartender job!"

Sharon grabbed Leon's hand explaining. "I have saved my annual leave up as well so that I could enjoy a while away from my work also, the advertisement said that they have got all of the players now and you wouldn't have wanted to enter into the game because it sounds extra cruel!"

Leon scratched his head. "Yes, I agree with cruel because it sounds brutal!"

Sharon nodded. "It also said that it is for adults only to watch with an orange button that can help or hinder!"

Leon sounded puzzled. "The orange button sounds interesting if it can do that!"

Sharon nodded. "Yeah, I agree, it sounds really strange but cool in a helpful way!"

Leon laughed. "It sounds like a hard game to play with difficult obstacles to deal with and maybe some adult content, I am just thinking about why dolls are never pregnant, I think the answer is because the male came in another box?"

Sharon chuckled slightly, then looked and sounded a little sad. "When it advertised the pain game on the television, it mentioned that the players can take six items each with them as they walk in, they are then injected by a pain enhancer needle that affects your pain area in the brain, the injection makes you have the worst ever pain that you will experience in your life from birth to now from head to toe!"

Leon sounded shocked. "Why would anyone want to do that to other people? I don't get why people would want to go through that; life is too short to be frightened for your life?"

Sharon sounded sad. "Because people are cruel, and some are desperate for money!"

Leon raised his hand, waving it about. "Well, everyone needs more money, going to work is our option for getting money, annoyingly, some people get paid to stay at home because they know how to swindle the government system, even if they are not entitled to the money, and they get away without doing a day's work in their entire lives!"

Sharon smiled. "Well, the contestants that enter into the pain game receive a needle that injects a fluid into their body, as it accelerates through their veins into their blood, the contestants get every pain all at once that they have ever had in their entire past life immediately after being injected!"

Leon sniffled. "So, the injection brings every pain back into your here and now, it will affect your whole body and change your life for the worst for six weeks including emotionally, physically, bruising, operations, stabbings, falling etc and anything and everything else that heals as naturally as it did back then as the injury had freshly happened!"

Sharon nodded up and down. "Yeah, that sums it all up!"

Leon sounded disturbed. "Niall Orange has just announced that the injection has got some kind of control over their minds as well as to control their body movements!"

Sharon looked at Niall Orange. "It sounds like Niall Orange has got no care for the contestants because he says that he is looking forward to a fierce battle for the contestants to stay alive!"

Leon let go of Sharon's hand and asked. "So, whoever is still alive, and, in the game, they win after being there for six weeks, endearing the worst situation that will affect the rest of their lives with them experiencing life and death dramatic and traumatic devastating moments?"

Sharon nodded yes. "Yes, that is correct, and it sounds like they will get more sex than I am getting, I need oiling up soon, and I am already twenty-five, and I am still waiting for happiness to happen in my life!"

Leon sounded upset. "I suppose it is to entertain people with sick minds; I am glad that I am not in the pain game, and I am just watching from home as a spectator away from harm, we are both the same age then and in the same situation!"

Sharon pondered. "This is a good but strange result!"

Leon nodded. "In my judgment, you are the perfect partner because you are soft, kindhearted, loving and beautifully attractive!"

Sharon fluttered her eyelashes and explained. "Thank you, it said on an advertisement on television the other day that when people enter the game between half an hour and an hour into the start of the game, they get the pain starting from what has previously happened to them until they leave the game at the end of six weeks with their body healing as it did as it happened back in that time of their lives that the pain was caused!"

Leon pulled a startled face. "I am going to have to watch this on television when it starts, what is it called, and when does it start, I am intrigued to find out more?"

Sharon sounded informative. "It is called the pain game, and it starts at nine pm tonight, and it finishes at ten pm, I am starting to feel so fired up to enjoy watching it!"

Leon smiled. "Me too, and I am just thinking, you should never trust stairs because they are always up to something!"

Sharon nodded. "True, you are daft!"

Leon glanced at Sharon's phone. "Socials are doing a live feed, is that the contestants in their red jackets?"

Sharon looked down at her phone. "Yes, it must be, they are all complimenting each other how nice each other look and how nice they smell!"

Leon looked at their names on the back of the contestant's jackets. "They will not look and smell nice when they leave the hotel and arrive in the unpredictable jungle!"

Sharon nodded up and down. "Yes, I think you are correct!"

Leon smirked, begging. "Can I please come and watch the pain game with you at your house Sharon, if we like watching it we could gift some money to the players in the game for being brave for being there!"

Sharon gasped. "I don't want to admit this, but I think that we are the sick ones watching it now!"

Leon sounded grateful. "Yes, I suppose we are the sick ones in the head, I will turn up at your front door just before the pain game starts at nine pm!"

Leon and Sharon walked home from the crumb sandwich shop in their own separate ways.

Sharon's doorbell rang with her answering her front door with a smile and a raised eyebrow, inviting Leon inside just before nine pm. "Come in Leon and make yourself at home with a beer from my fridge!"

Chapter Two

Pain Enhancing Needle

Leon walked in and sat down on the sofa and got comfortable. "You smell as sweet as flowers, and you have got the warmest smile that is as bright and as wide as the sun that could warm and melt anyones heart, and you need to sit down Sharon because they're playing the dramatic music that sounds like a violin!"

Sharon slurped her beer. "Oh look, they are all getting injected with the pain enhancer needle as they are about to walk into the jungle, I wouldn't want to be them right now, I am so happy that Sophie Ball and Niall Orange are the voice-overs for the game, they are my favourite people that used to play the characters in the film Dream Changing, they look well dressed in nice clothes as usual!"

Leon watched the players signing their consent forms. "It says on their consent forms that they have got to write down who their dead bodies should go to if the worst happens!"

Sharon pulled a startled face. "That's a bit disturbing, to say the least!"

Leon kissed Sharon on the cheek. "Yes, I agree, and I hope that you don't mind me kissing you?"

Sharon glowed with happiness. "Of course, you need to kiss me more often because you make my heart skip a beat!"

Leon looked in detail at the television. "I like the fact that the contestants have all got microphones on the top of their clothes, and the microphones look like a tiny fluffy badge near to their mouths so that we can hear everything that they are saying, this is so cool!"

Sharon sounded concerned. "They all look scared and in pain already from their injection because they are nursing different parts of their bodies, in fact, it looks like they are in the worst pain that they have experienced in their lives!"

Leon shook his head from side to side. "God help them because it is only the start of week one, and I love the sweet sound of the violins playing in the background with it signalling the start of the game, I do feel a little bit sorry for them, and I am jealous at the same time because someone will win the enormous money jackpot if any of them do survive their living nightmare!"

Sharon smirked. "Yeah, that is true!"

Leon stared at the screen. "What a great idea, look, they have got their names on the front and back of their red coats in large writing and also on their transparent rucksacks!"

Sharon's eyes lit up brightly. "I guess their names are printed, so that it is clear who they are and nothing can be hidden, and they all sound like they are regretting being there already with them moaning about the explosion of pain hitting them all at once from their head to their feet, I wouldn't want to experience this!"

Leon shook his head from side to side. "I am glad that I am here safe with you, I feel like the luckiest man alive to be by your side!"

Sharon looked at Amelia's name on her red coat. "Amelia is moaning about how hard it was to win the tug of war that they had to win to enter into the game!"

Leon nodded up and down. "Yeah, and Benjamin is looking around and calling it a death trap that they have volunteered to enter into!"

Sharon sounded optimistic. "Well, they have got no choice but to get on with the game, because sadly for them, there's no option for them to get back onto the plane to go home now to get away from the dangers in the jungle!"

Leon smirked. "I can't believe a tug of war was the decider of going into the jungle, or the opposite option was for them to stay at home!"

Sharon looked at Leon. "I can't believe it either, look, they are playing the tug of war in the background that previously happened on a large screen!"

Leon looked back at Sharon. "The results were so close, it quite easily could have been the opposition team winning instead, it sounds like they were lucky to win!"

Sharon pointed. "Look, all the pain game contestants look so young, they don't look above twenty years old any of them!"

Leon agreed. "Wow, yes, now that I am looking around at them all, they do look very young, I bet that's why they are in the pain game so that they can retire, if I ever start complaining that any music is too loud it means that I am probably getting too old!"

Niall Orange and Sophie Ball discuss that the contestants look eager to give it a go with Sharon glaring in more detail. "Oh yes, at least if their faces get unrecognisably mangled so that we don't see their unique features anymore, we will still know who they are as long as their names on their red coats don't get damaged too badly, and we all hopefully grow old!"

Leon sounded upset. "I feel sorry for their parents if they do lose their lives!"

Sharon had tears in her eyes. "Yes, that would be devastating!"

Leon was in deep thought. "I am just thinking, do you know why the skeleton had to put his coat on?"

Sharon raised her shoulders. "I don't know the answer!"

Leon answered. "Because he was chilled to the bones!"

Sharon laughed. "You are funny, Leon!"

Leon pointed out the eight contestants' names on the screen. "Look, Amelia looks like she is crying with her whole body in pain from the pain-enhancing needle already bringing back every pain that she ever had in her life all at once!"

Amelia cries speaking. "I feel frightened, but this is something that I have got to do!"

Sharon crossed her legs on the sofa. "It looks like Amelia is Chinese with bright blue eyes like the sea behind her spectacles, if she survives, I bet she could make a good Chinese curry, she looks like she is regretting going into the game already with her looking so petrified and pale in the face and the weather looks like it is a mixed bag with it raining and sunny at the same time!"

Leon has a scrunched-up puzzled face. "They all look like they are in excruciating pain after the needle touched them, and there are no toilets or showers for them to use making it an uninhabitable and unhygienic place!"

Sharon pointed at the sky on the television. "The game players will be very sensitive to the bright lights with no sunglasses on to protect their eyes from the bright sun solar system in the sky!"

Leon scrunched up his eyes. "I never remove my sunglasses when the sun shines because my eyes are so sensitive, and I bet sunglasses need a vacation to relax their frame of mind!"

Sharon had a shiver down her spine, smirking. "I would feel so grubby without a regular proper wash in the jungle because it looks so dusty and dirty, and it is very loud with animals all around, the weather and the sound of drones rolling or walking around can be annoyingly loud!"

Leon held his hands together. "Me too, I don't like feeling dirty either and yes, the noise levels are very elevated!"

Sharon sounded a little bit more comforted. "Look, Niall Orange is reassuring Amelia that she is playing the game for the money and no other reason, and they could help each other out and share the money between them or the opposite!"

Amelia whispered to herself. "I am going to give this game all I can give to win the jackpot, even if it means playing rough, and I think that a bit of rain is nice and cooling!"

Leon giggled to himself. "If I died, I would travel towards the light, I am that tight with money, I would turn it off!"

Sharon smiled. "You have got some silly jokes!"

Leon laughed. "I bet Niall Orange and Sophie Ball wouldn't want to go into the game themselves as a contestant!"

Sharon played with her hands. "Yeah, they look like they look after themselves too much with everything prim and proper with not a hair out of place with all of their bells and whistles to make them look pristine!"

Leon chuckled. "Niall Orange and Sophie Ball do look a little bit stuck up their own arses and snobby!"

Chapter Three

One Eye Open

A red drone rolled over to the contestants speaking. "I will only tell you this once so listen carefully and do not forget, if you need a safe place for two days only in the last week of the pain game, there is one available, but my rule is that you can only enter into the secret room for safety as a team with whoever is left, firstly you would need to find the secret orange access card that will appear in the haunted house for you to find so that you can swipe it on the way in to open the door, but I repeat, it will only appear on the last week and you are not exempt from our activities!"

The red drone rolled away with Sharon smiling. "Oh heck, that sounds like a haven for them to go to, and do you know why cows wear bells?"

Leon had a clueless look. "I wish that I knew!"

Sharon answered. "Because their horns don't work!"

Leon grinned. "Very good, I am impressed!"

Sharon gave her opinion. "I think as the game goes on, people will drop out because they won't be able to cope with the pain, they will hurt each other to win a larger amount of money if the animals or whatever else doesn't kill them first!"

Leon sounded surprised. "Sophie Ball has just announced that they can cause more pain to each other, making it excruciating!"

Sharon stroked her fingers. "It sounds bad, but they could even kill each other by attacking one another, with them struggling to get away from each other as well as the game causing them plenty of drama!"

Leon raised his eyebrows. "I think that there are many sick games ahead for them to deal with!"

Sharon looked in deep thought. "So, they are encouraging each other to steal each others items, which will make the game more interesting, as if it isn't already interesting enough with them being injected with the pain-enhancing needles!"

Leon looked in deep thought. "Well, I am just thinking that I would compliment a well-threaded needle by saying that they are really stitching things up good and proper!"

Sharon coughed with a smile, sounding surprised. "I am shocked that Amelia's six items that she has chosen are a sleeping bag, tarpaulin for shelter, a knife, a fishing rod, a bow and arrow and a first aid kit!"

Amelia whispered to herself. "I just hope that I have got enough ammunition to keep me alive!"

Leon looked open-mouthed. "I would want to take a needle into the game as well to stab someone with the needle to inflict pain on anyone that wanted to hurt me!"

Sharon's eyes lit up. "Yes, I really do think that a needle would give me a few extra, more survivable options!"

Leon sounded interested. "Listen, Sophie Ball is wishing them all luck, and Niall Orange is encouraging them to carry on until the end, and there may be a needle in Amelia's first aid kit to stitch her damaged skin up, if she needs it!"

Sharon agreed. "Yes, and they are saying it like they have got a choice, once they walk into the pain game and receive their pain enhancer needle in their arm, that is the start of the game with no going back for six weeks!"

Leon pointed out. "They have just gone in as they are because they have all got similar red warm coats on, so the coats are obviously not part of the six items aloud because they were provided by the pain game show!"

Sharon pointed at the trees on the television. "The only way for them to keep safe is for them to climb up the trees etc to try to keep safe, or they could end up with an axe in their heads!"

Leon pulled a strange face. "That's if it doesn't rain, making it too slippery to climb the trees, and I am just thinking, trees are some of the best networks because they branch out well!"

Sharon smirked, pointing out Benjamin going near to the haunted house. "Did you see that?"

Benjamin was about to set up his base at the side of the haunted house until he nearly got a knife in his head from an open window above!"

Benjamin drew a cross on his chest. "Wow, that was too close!"

Leon gasped. "Yes, that was a close call, Benjamin was nearly a goner, that must be one of the dangers in the haunted house, and he is struggling to walk, he must have broken his leg at some point in his past life, and Sophie Ball is talking about all of the money that they can win!"

Sharon's eyes glimmered. "Benjamin's eyes are a lovely light green colour; it would have been a shame to lose them!"

Leon rubbed his eye. "I hope my eyes are around for a long time, and I am just thinking that opticians and teachers have a lot in common because they both like testing people!"

Sharon's eyes lit up, grinning. "Yes, eight billion pounds is a staggering amount of money for them to share between whoever is left at the end of the pain game still playing on the last day of the six weeks, Niall Orange has just said!"

Leon had his ears pricked open. "Sophie Ball has just announced that the pain before they got their inflicted pain needle will disappear again when they receive their reverse pain needle, that needle will make them go back to how they were before they entered the game!"

Sharon struggled to understand. "Yes, but the new pain that's been inflicted on their bodies during the game will still stand!"

Leon nodded up and down. "That is difficult for them!"

Sharon laughed. "Yes, it will, and by the look of it, Benjamin is from America with his accent, he has got a candle, matches, tarpaulin, a pillow, a knife and a sleeping bag, I don't think he will be doing much sleeping, he will permanently have one eye open on guard!"

Benjamin spoke to himself. "What have I let myself in for?"

Leon agreed. "I wouldn't feel like sleeping at all if I were in that situation that Benjamin is in!"

Sharon glanced at the players. "They look so cold, vulnerable and frightened!"

Chapter Four

Survival

Leon pointed at Drew as he got covered by a man-made snow avalanche. "I bet Drew is so cold because he is shivering so badly with the bits I can see poking out of the snow, his brown eyes look so frightened, it is a good job that he has got his hood up, that may have saved him, and all Niall Orange can talk about is if Drew is alive!"

Drew's teeth chattered, struggling to speak. "I really need to warm up, and I am struggling to stand up with it being so slippery underfoot!"

Sharon looked at Drew sadly. "Sophie Ball has noticed and announced that Drew is okay, I bet Drew will probably have frost-bite, and he is struggling to carry his belongings possibly because he is so cold, he has just tipped them out onto the floor, he has got a pan, a bar of soap, a pocketknife, a sleeping bag, a sewing kit and a hot water bottle!"

Leon nodded yes. "I agree, Drew will probably have frostbite because he is so slim as well, and it sounds like he has got some useful items, and I think Drew is from South Africa from his accent that I am picking up, he is very lucky that he has not slipped on the solid frozen hard ground!"

Sharon smiled. "Drew will be used to being warm, not cold, and he is filling his pan with loose snow; it must be so that he can have a drink later, and Sophie Ball is praising Drew for thinking on his feet!"

Leon watched Drew in detail. "I don't know how he is going to warm his water because he doesn't have any way of lighting a fire unless he uses two sticks!"

Sharon sounded very interested. "I find that really strange because Drew is walking behind Benjamin; he must be wanting to steal something from him!"

Leon agreed. "I guess so, Drew is hiding behind a large tree because Benjamin has sat down on the floor!"

Sharon stared at Drew. "Ooh, look, how naughty, Drew is trying to look in Benjamin's bag while he isn't looking!"

Leon gasped. "No surprise there, but Benjamin Is shaking with anger, and he looks like he is foaming at the mouth with aggression because he has just yelled at Drew!"

Sharon sounded stern. "I would be furious as well if I were Benjamin, he sounds scary the way that he is threatening Drew to leave his bag alone or he would kill him, and Niall

Orange is also pointing out the violence between Benjamin and Drew!"

Leon pointed at Benjamin. "He looks like he is going to cry!"

Sharon was involved. "That's odd, Benjamin has got a brown eye and a blue eye, did you notice?"

Leon smiled. "Yeah, it is different!"

Sharon sounded surprised. "Drew has run off, and by the look of it, he has managed to get a match from Benjamin's bag, and he is lighting a fire, and Sophie Ball is saying how brave Drew is for stealing a match from Benjamin with him still being high rate, at least on the upside it is not raining!"

Leon pointed out. "At least Drew can try to get warm because he has put the water in his hot water bottle to keep him warm as well as his fire that is starting to burn well!"

Sharon laughed at Emma. "At least Drew will be a little warmer, and I think that Emma has got no chance of winning, she has got a mirror probably to look at herself, a lipstick, a sleeping bag, a torch, tarpaulin and a pan and I think she sounds like she is from Yorkshire in the United Kingdom judging from her accent and her light brown eyes look so nice!"

Leon sounded surprised. "You may be wrong about Emma because she is using the reflection of the sun on the mirror to try to set some kindling on fire to keep her warm, and the lipstick looks like a secret knife under the lid, and she is looking in the mirror for any strange activity behind her!"

Sharon sounded surprised. "I suppose Emma has got more brains sense than she looks like she has got with her looking pretty as a picture, Sophie Ball also sounds surprised at how Emma had a good idea to survive!"

Emma looked at herself in her mirror. "I am going to survive this game and win the jackpot!"

Leon started to look at Marie. "Marie looks like a stocky lady, her extra tummy pounds will go against her because it could slow her down, and she has got pretty light blue eyes, she needs to keep moving forward so that she doesn't get caught by any unwanted sharp as a knife attention heading her way!"

Sharon sounded intrigued. "Marie has got a pen, paper, tarpaulin, scissors, a pan, and a sleeping bag and she sounds like she's a Brummie from Birmingham with her accent, and do you know what you call a skeleton with a mask and a knife?"

Leon asked the answer. "I don't know!"

Sharon announced. "The answer is a heartless killer!"

Leon's jaw dropped. "That was good!"

Sharon sounded happy. "Thank you, Leon, I am glad you liked my joke!"

Leon sounded surprised. "I think that Marie is so tall I bet she bangs her head all the time, Niall Orange is commenting how tall Marie is, and he could do with Marie nearby permanently to reach things from the top shelf for him sometimes!"

Marie spoke to herself. "Hopefully, with my fast thinking, I will push through the pain to the end!"

Sharon's eyes fixed on Brandon. "Wow, Brandon looks sweaty and unwell, he is a good-looking fit man with him breaking down like ice cream not kept in the freezer because he keeps crying!"

Leon pointed at Brandon. "Brandon has got a fishing rod, a torch, gloves, a pan, a sleeping bag and a small pop-up tent, and yes, he does look like a broken car that can't be fixed at the moment!"

Sharon sounded surprised. "Brandon has got a Scottish accent; I love this accent, and his hazel eyes look cute!"

Leon's eyes lit up suggesting. "We should go to Scotland together one day, it is supposed to be a great place to visit!"

Brandon wiped a tear from his eye. "This is such a stressful time, I am not sure if I can do this, but I will muddle through for the large money reward for staying here for six weeks!"

Sharon pointed at Ava. "Ava sounds scared and worried talking to herself saying that she just needs to kill the other contestants, then survive for six weeks, and Sophie Ball is commenting that Ava may change her mind about killing others if she gets to know them or she may go the other way and be more eager to kill others around her!"

Leon looked at Ava's rook sack. "Ava has got a first aid kit, a pair of scissors, a knife, a fishing rod, a pan and a pop-up tent that may keep her warmer, but definitely not safer!"

Ava softly spoke to herself, sounding distressed. "I have got a feeling that this place isn't very safe, and if anyone is nice to me, I will be nice back to keep myself alive!"

Sharon shrugged her shoulders. "Well, I am surprised that Ava doesn't have a sleeping bag so that she could use it as a seat, or to keep her warm!"

Leon sounded surprised. "Niall Orange is commenting how he likes Ava's Spanish accent, her sky-blue eyes and how she speaks English so well, I bet Niall likes Ava a bit more than as just a contestant!"

Sharon agreed. "Yes, Niall is right, Ava does speak excellent English, and she sounds like a breath of fresh air, and she makes me feel relaxed when she speaks, it sounds like Sophie Ball also likes Ava as much as Niall Orange because they are talking about her lovely accent and calm manner as well!"

Chapter Five

Romance In The Air

Leon sounded scared for Joseph. "Joseph is walking along in the middle of a rainstorm that is over his head, I would feel so worried if I were him, and he just sounds happy to have his coat on, and do you know what a pile of coins is called in a rainstorm?"

Sharon looked puzzled. "I don't know!"

Leon laughed, speaking. "Climate change!"

Sharon chuckled, glancing at Joseph's bag. "I am surprised that Joseph has got a whistle. He will not use that because it will draw attention to himself!"

Leon pointed at Joseph's bag. "Joseph has also got a pan, matches, a book, a small tent, and a fishing rod as well as his whistle, and Sophie Ball has just mentioned that she loves Josephs Italian accent and his dark blue eyes because she thinks that it sounds sexy!"

Joseph sounded thankful. "I am glad that I have got my coat right now!"

Sharon pointed at the floor. "I have just noticed that Brandon is trying to fish in very shallow waters using his fishing rod, I hope for his sake that he catches some fish!"

Leon sounded positive. "Brandon is walking along the lake bottom with uneven surfaces under his feet with only a trickle of water flowing with the sun beating down on them all, making them hot, and he has removed his coat because the sun is shining brightly!"

Sharon sounded upset, sniffling. "I think that Emma is trying to get Brandon out of the game so that she has got more money because she is staring at him in deep thought, like she is planning something bad!"

Leon shouted. "You need to turn around Brandon now, or it looks like you will get panned to death and floored in a minute by Emma, and Niall Orange sounds like he is getting excited about what is happening!"

Sharon sounded in shock. "Emma has just hit Brandon on the back of his head with her pan, he looks to be in so much pain with him holding his head, I think that he looks to be in a daze!"

Leon pointed. "Look, Brandon has passed out onto the floor!"

Sharon sounded a little traumatised. "Brandon looks like he is dead because he is lifeless, and nobody is helping him. Oh heck, Sophie Ball is already ruling him out of the game!"

Leon pointed at Brandon. "Nobody will help him because they are all just after the fight to win the money, and yes, I think that Brandon must be dead because he isn't moving a muscle!"

Sharon looked at Brandon. "Maybe, look, Niall Orange has suddenly dropped silent!"

Leon watched Niall. "I guess that Niall is wondering if Brandon is alive!"

Sharon agreed. "Amelia is still rubbing her body better; I feel sorry for her being in so much pain, and Sophie Ball is looking at Amelia sadly, feeling glad that she isn't in Amelia's unbearable painful body!"

Leon's eyes nearly popped out of his sockets. "Look, Brandon is starting to move, he is trying to get up, Emma's walked off, and Amelia is standing looking over Brandon pointing her bow and arrow at

Brandon's head and by the sound of it Niall Orange is celebrating that Brandon has come around as well!"

Sharon sounded shocked. "Amelia looks like she must have pain in her foot because she walks very slowly like it's painful underfoot, and I think that Amelia feels like she can't shoot Brandon with her arrow!"

Leon sounded sad. "I would probably feel terribly guilty killing someone on purpose as well because their family would lose a precious family member and look, Sophie Ball looks completely relieved that Amelia can't shoot Brandon because she's holding her head in her hands!"

Sharon sounded gobsmacked. "I can't believe it; Amelia is helping Brandon up from the floor, and Brandon has just kissed her cheek, Niall Orange is announcing that there may be a romance in the air!"

Brandon speaks to Amelia. "Your cheek is so soft and warm, thank you for sparing my life, I really do appreciate that!"

Amelia wiped a tear with her fingers. "I just couldn't kill you, it felt wrong to hurt you; I think that we should all be able to share the money in the end!"

Brandon cuddled Amelia. "I am behind you if you need my help, and you have got such a pretty face that is a work of art!"

Leon stared at the television screen. "At least Amelia has explained to Brandon that she just wants to get through the six weeks, and she wants to commit the perfect crime by stealing each others' hearts!"

Sharon sounded a little sad. "I think that's so sweet, look, Brandon has just kissed her on the cheek again, and he has thanked Amelia for not killing him, I can't wait for the next episode tomorrow, the first of this day's episode has finished, and I can't wait for the second episode tomorrow!"

Niall Orange and Sophie Ball talk about a wind-up tiny gold clock that is hidden in the jungle, when it's wound up, it has got a digging-out motion that is a good tool for whoever finds it.

Leon looked at Niall Orange and Sophie Ball, discussing the tiny wind-up gold clock. "I really do hope that they find it, and do you know why toilets are so good at poker?"

Sharon danced a jig to the violins, signalling that it was the end. "I don't know, and I just thought that I would have a silly dance!"

Leon sounded positive. "Toilets always get a flush and the pain game is nicely turning us on, it must be watching people in pain that is doing it, and I could give you a back massage if you like, but I would need to at least remove your top so that it would be like you have got a bikini on!"

Sharon asked Leon. "With your stunning body, I know that it won't just be a back massage because I will not be able to resist your body, and do you want to stay the night in my bed with me, we don't have to go near each other if you don't want to, and a back massage sounds really good!"

Leon nodded, giving Sharon a gentle kiss on the cheek. "You are tempting me so much, and yes; I am definitely up for satisfying us both, even though it is late now!"

Sharon asked. "Do you want to go up to bed now because I am tired?"

Leon nodded up and down. "I feel tired as well!"

Sharon stood up. "I am just going to get some olive oil to see if it will sort my squeaky bed out, and I love the way that you look at me like I look at chocolate cake with your puppy dog eyes!"

Chapter Six

Tickle Truncheon

Leon followed Sharon upstairs, speaking. "I feel like we get on very well because all we do is chat to each other like best friends do, and has anyone ever told you that your long blonde hair looks amazingly soft and bouncy with it being slightly curly?"

Sharon sat on the bed fully clothed. "Thank you for your compliment, and I really could do with a cuddle to make me feel cosier and like I am not alone!"

Leon smiled. "I can definitely oblige to that, but we could do to remove our clothes and put something more comfortable on!"

Sharon walked into the bathroom and changed into her short candy floss pink silky nightgown. "I am much comfier now!"

Leon shouted from the bathroom. "I will be with you shortly, my darling!"

Sharon looked at the door, waiting in anticipation and excitement, listening for the knob on the bathroom door to turn. "Please don't be long, my cuteness!"

Leon stripped off to his underpants and got into bed. "Now that I am laid at the side of you, all I can think of is stripping your nightgown off with my teeth so that I touch your lovely naked body!"

Sharon turned the light off, speaking. "I think that would be really nice, the thought of laying next to your well-toned up muscly fit body turns me on big time!"

Leon sounded happy. "I wasn't expecting that reply, but it is the reply that I have dreamt of coming out of your mouth!"

Sharon sounded grateful. "I think we have both wanted this intimate moment for a while!"

Leon started to gently tickle Sharon's legs using his soft, warm, and long fingers. "Does that feel good, Sharon?"

Sharon sighed. "Oh yeah, it is doing the trick for me, is that your own personal tickle truncheon stick that I can feel trapped that's trying to break free?"

Leon sounded excited. "Yes, you can release it if you like so that I can spank you with it!"

Sharon helped to release the beast. "You feel so firm and hard as a rock, please, tickle me with your beast that I have released!"

Leon poured some olive oil onto his penis, then rubbed his tickling stick up and down Sharon's legs. "I feel like I need to fill you with my joyful wand!"

Sharon opened her legs wide. "Go for it, I need this, kiss me like you have never kissed before!"

Leon thrusted inside of Sharon. "You feel lovely and tightly warm squeezing my penis inside of your wet, inviting clit!"

Sharon sounded joyful. "You are making me feel so excited, you feel so smooth thrusting fast inside of me, and you are filling my vagina with warmth and passion!"

Leon cuddled his arms around Sharon. "I am about to spray my love juices inside of you because I can't hold them back any longer because your body feels amazing!"

Sharon screamed. "I can feel your juices penetrating inside of me, it feels amazing!"

Leon laid down at the side of Sharon. "I really enjoyed that, let's fall asleep cuddling each other, we can keep each other warm!"

Sharon laid down on the bed and then kissed Leon on the cheek. "Good night!"

Leon woke up first and made Sharon a coffee. "Let's watch some films and go for lunch at the Crumbs sandwich shop until the pain game starts at nine pm!"

Sharon sounded happy as it turned nine pm. "The second episode of the pain game is just starting now with the violins playing softly, and Ava has just left her pop-up tent, it looks like she is in pain with her stomach because she is doubled over crying, and she looks so frightened with her holding her knife!"

Leon screamed. "It's a good job that Ava has got her knife handy because a snake is about to bite her leg, she has stabbed the snake very quickly!"

Sharon sounded relieved. "Yes, that was a close call, it is a good job that Ava reacted fast, at least she can eat the snake now instead of being bitten, she is moaning about the pain from her having her gallbladder removed in the past, it is a good job that she wasn't bitten, or it would be real life pain and old injuries from her pain enhancing injection!"

Leon sounded content. "Ava is trying to light a fire unsuccessfully using two pieces of wood. Oh, wait a minute, I think that it has lit with her bits of kindling starting to burn, and I bet the extra pain inflicted onto them is really getting to them!"

Ava sounded proud. "I knew that I could light it because I can turn my hand to most skills, personally I love trying to reach out my talents!"

Sharon pointed. "Look, Joseph has just blown his whistle in Ava's ear, I bet that was deafening because she jumped that much, if you noticed, she nearly hit the clouds in the sky! "

Leon sounded shocked. "Ava has looked around, and she has just smacked Joseph in the face, and look, his nose is bleeding everywhere, Sophie Ball is commenting on the huge amount of blood leaving his nose!"

Sharon gasped. "Ewe, blood is dripping down onto Joseph's jumper, I bet he has got a broken nose because the blood is coming out so fast, like a waterfall, and his nose is looking crooked!"

Joseph's eyes were severely watering, and his nose was bloody. "I know that I probably deserved that, but I think that you must have definitely broken my nose, Ava, because it's really painful!"

Leon sounded surprised. "Marie is stealing Ava's snake now that it's sizzling and cooked and ready to eat using her scissors as a fork!"

Sharon laughed. "That sounds a bit funny when you said a snake, I was thinking of something else that is in your underwear, and Marie has run off and Ava is chasing Marie, and Ava has caught Marie up pulling Marie's hair!"

Marie whispered to herself. "Well, I nearly had some fresh meat that was cooked for me, and it smelt so delicious, and it was in touching distance!"

Chapter Seven

Bedroom Antics

Leon smirked. "Marie looks like she is crying in pain in her back because of the way that she is struggling to walk, and at least Ava has got her food back, and Marie has given in and run off, or she has tried to with her being a little stocky!"

Sharon sounded a little sad. "Marie looks hungry because she is rubbing her stomach, and she must have hurt her back in the past!"

Leon noticed and pointed out. "Look, a parcel that is rattling loudly in the shape of a large leaf is falling from the sky, and Amelia is walking towards it first, I bet it is full of food!"

Sharon sounded surprised. "Amelia has opened the leaf bag up, and I really can't believe this because it's full of vodka, I think this will make the game more interesting with alcohol on the agenda and not much available to eat!"

Leon raised his eyebrows. "Yes, we will find out if they turn a little mushy or aggressive with each other shortly!"

Sharon sounded surprised. "Marie is walking towards Amelia!"

Leon gasped. "Marie and Amelia are sharing the vodka out between them like civilised people; they may not be civilised when they have finished drinking all of the vodka though!"

Marie drank some vodka. "At least we can enjoy the moment while it lasts!"

Amelia nodded up and down. "Yes, I totally agree, let's enjoy ourselves and get tipsy!"

Sharon pointed at Marie. "Look, Marie has got some chocolate bars from the leaf bag, and Drew is marching fast towards Marie, and Amelia is licking her lips, Drew is so slim he will need plenty of food to keep him going!"

Leon laughed. "The chocolate may sober them up a little bit, and I am glad that we will not get Marie, and Amelia's headaches from all of the vodka being drunk, and I am just thinking, the suns favourite chocolate is the Milky Way!"

Sharon smiled, reaching for her beer. "Me too, and that's strange having random interesting facts hovering from large boards from different trees around the forest!"

Leon rolled his eyes. "Nothing surprises me at all here, and I didn't know that the Amazon rain forest is six-point seven square kilometres, that's twice the size of India or twenty-eight times the size of the United Kingdom, you learn something new every day!"

Sharon opened her mouth in awe. "Wow, that's very big!"

Leon sounded informative. "They all look interested by the boards because the players are looking upwards at them!"

Sharon raised her eyebrows. "I would be interested to read the boards as well because it is something different to look at, I suppose!"

Leon moaned. "I feel devastated because episode two of the pain game has finished on the first week already, and none of them found the tiny wind-up gold clock!"

Sharon sounded a little sad. "We will have to wait until nine pm tomorrow for more excitement in the jungle, and don't worry, someone will find the clock!"

Leon turned the television off. "I am picking you up Sharon, and I am carrying you to your bedroom, this moment feels so special!"

Leon carried Sharon upstairs. "Will you start by giving me a foot massage, Leon?"

Leon smiled. "I will do anything for you Sharon, because you are my world!"

Sharon stripped naked and then jumped into bed. "That feels lovely, tranquil and relaxing, Leon!"

Leon sounded happy. "I am moving upwards towards your smooth hair free clit!"

Sharon moaned. "This feels so amazing, did you know that my clit is the most sensitive part of my body when you touch it?"

Leon laughed. "I guessed so; it will have so many triggers from my penis filling every part of your vagina walls in a minute!"

Sharon closed her eyes with her unable to stop moaning. "I really do love your body; you turn me on so much like a clock!"

Leon lay next to Sharon, speaking. "Being laid next to your beautiful warm naked body is turning me on so much, your breasts are so hard, but your skin feels so warm and soft, and your inviting clit is so tight and wet!"

Sharon dragged Leon's fingers towards her clit speaking. "Your amazing magical fingers are making me cum so much!"

Leon moved his fingers inside and out of her clit, fast. "You are so wet, and I am getting so hot, my penis loves pinging up to attention when I am near you!"

Sharon demanded. "Sit on my face, and I will suck your cock!"

Leon apologised. "I am sorry Sharon, but I am ejaculating into your mouth!"

Sharon swallowed and then spoke. "You will have to fill my anus next with your warm creamy spunky juices, and in our future lives, even if it rains, or pours, I am all yours and always there for you through sickness and health!"

Leon stroked Sharon's hair. "I feel the same way about you!"

Sharon crossed her arms. "I am glad that you feel the same, I think that we make a sweet couple together!"

Leon sounded gooey. "You are my rock!"

Sharon sounded in love. "You are my open book that we can spend the rest of our life writing together that is waiting for us to write our love story to tell our future children!"

Leon sounded loved. "It will be the best love story ever, I am sure!"

Sharon kissed Leon on his cheek. "I will always love you!"

Leon agreed kissing Sharon back, and they slept, they then enjoyed a walk the next day until episode three started with Sharon on the edge of her seat speaking. "I wonder what will happen tonight, and the violins sound very upbeat?"

Leon listened to the violins. "The violins sound great!"

Sharon stared at the television. "We will find out in a minute what is about to happen!"

Leon looked at a board hovering from a tree. "I can't believe that the Amazon jungle is home to ten percent of all known species on earth, and every day there is a new species of animal or plant found!"

Sharon's eyes widened. "This is so interesting to know, and Marie and Amelia look like they are sober now!"

Leon listened to the introduction recap. "We will find out now!"

Sharon pointed out a piano. "Look, a piano has appeared in the jungle, I guess that it is some kind of trap!"

Leon sounded shocked. "The piano has obviously appeared from nowhere with a sign saying somebody that plays it will have a chance of being hurt or even killed, I hope that people notice that sign for their own sakes!"

Sharon agreed. "The sign should be a little larger really, but at least it is a sign, and it is better than some street and road signs, I noticed a road sign called Bell End the other day in Worcestershire, it cracked me up! "

Leon laughed. "Marie and Amelia don't look very civilised now because they look angry trying to climb a tree, I guess that they are probably still tipsy from the vodka that they drank!"

Sharon pointed at Joseph. "Joseph is about to sit at the piano, and I am just thinking, a piano can always get out of jail because it has got plenty of keys to hand!"

Leon convulsed with laughing. "Yes, strangely, Joseph has just got catapulted from his piano seat!"

Sharon giggled. "I can't control my laughter because Joseph has just landed on top of Ava!"

Chapter Eight

Illuminating Situation

Leon sounded serious. "Ava has just hit Joseph in his eye, and it looks red and painful!"

Ava shook her head. "Trust you to land on me!"

Joseph struggled to get off Ava. "I was out of control; I do apologise Ava, and you have hurt me again!"

Sharon gasped. "So, Ava has busted Joseph's nose and his eye now!"

Leon nodded yes. "Joseph is also complaining about a pain in his mouth, he must have had an abscess, or something at some point earlier in his life that is giving him pain again from the injection he received as he walked into the jungle!"

Sharon had her eyes on Brandon. "Brandon looks like his head is still hurting from Emma hitting him with a pan earlier because he keeps rubbing it!"

Leon stared at Marie. "Marie has just found a large chocolate cake behind a tree, and Brandon is walking towards Marie licking his lips!"

Sharon gasped. "Look, Brandon is stomping towards Marie!"

Leon smiled. "Marie has smothered Brandon with her sleeping bag!"

Marie started eating the chocolate cake while still smothering Brandon. "This is the best-tasting chocolate cake that I have ever tasted!"

Sharon pointed at Drew, walking towards Brandon and Marie. "Drew has got a pan of warm water in one hand and his soap in his other hand, and he has just dipped his soap in the water, and he has put the pan down on the floor, what is he going to do with that do you think?"

Leon sounded shocked. "Drew has just wet his soap and rubbed it in Marie's eyes so that she could not follow Brandon, I don't think that it will wash either of their worries away!"

Sharon gasped, sniggering. "Marie has put the remaining half of her chocolate cake on her transparent rook sack, and Brandon has run off with her cake gasping for air, I am glad that Drew distracted Marie so that Brandon could get away!"

Leon stared at Drew. "Drew has just stopped Brandon from getting killed, and Drew has walked away from Marie, leaving her to try to wipe the soap out of her eyes, it must really sting!"

Sharon shouted. "Oh no, episode three is coming to an end!"

Leon moaned. "I can't wait for episode four tomorrow, and I can't believe nobody has found the clock again!"

Sharon sounded sad. "Me too, let's just cuddle for a while before we go to sleep!"

Leon put his arms around Sharon. "This is nice, I can feel my little man down there waking up to meet you!"

Sharon put her hands on Leon's penis. "That feels nice, and warm and solid, you are correct, he is saluting me!"

Leon smirked. "Your hands are making my penis stand up to attention even more!"

Sharon stripped off while Leon did at the same time, with Sharon speaking. "Please put your penis in between my breasts!"

Leon nodded yes. "I agree, this feels really nice in between your breasts!"

Sharon demanded. "Please put your penis inside of my vagina and fill every bit of me!"

Leon announced. "You don't have to ask me to do that twice, I am going in!"

Sharon groaned. "That's amazing, if you could get a degree at university for enjoying sex, you would get top marks or even a distinction because you deserve it!"

Leon proudly mentioned. "Thank you for that comment, I am ejaculating inside of you right now!"

Sharon smiled. "That felt amazing, thank you for filling me with your amazing warmth!"

Leon and Sharon turned the light off and slept, the next day they went to town to get some shopping until episode four of the pain game started with Leon sounding excited. "Episode four is about to start because the violins are playing again!"

Sharon's eyes were glued to the television screen, looking and sounding intrigued. "Amelia looks like she is crying, holding her fishing rod, looking up at a large whiteboard with black writing on it!"

Leon sounded distracted. "It says that the Amazon is home to forty-seven million people, including more than two million indigenous people, and it says that more than four hundred indigenous groups live in the Amazon, this is more than anywhere else on earth, and around three hundred indigenous languages are spoken throughout the Amazon!"

Sharon smirked. "I find these facts so interesting!"

Leon sounded a little sad! "Amelia is probably hungry by the look of it, that is possibly why she is crying!"

Sharon agreed. "Amelia needs to get some food from Brandon somehow!"

Leon pointed. "Emma is walking towards Amelia with her torch shining bright in the dark; I don't know if this is a good situation!"

Sharon pointed out. "This is an illuminating situation, and Emma has got her lipstick in her hand!"

Leon gasped. "Emma is upset because she is hungry as well because I can hear her stomach rumbling from here!"

Sharon mentioned. "Amelia has walked away from Emma!"

Leon smirked. "A large, tall, steep and long fun red slide has just appeared in between Emma and Amelia, that looks odd!"

Sharon's eyes nearly popped out of her sockets. "Wow, the slide towers over all of the trees, I can't believe how tall it is!"

Leon pointed at Emma. "Look, Emma is climbing up the steps to the slide, the steps look a little bit slippery because Emma's feet are sliding around!"

Emma whispered to herself. "That slide looks so cool; I need to try that out!"

Sharon sounded horrified. "Look, Emma is about to go down the terrifying high slide, and I know that something bad will happen to her, I don't know why, but I have got this horrible feeling more trouble is about to happen!"

Leon sounded appalled. "Emma looks excited, but I am sure your gut feeling is correct because nearly everything goes wrong in this game!"

Sharon sounded a little confused. "Emma has just started to go down the slide with her still being okay up to now!"

Leon spoke with gritted teeth. "Oh no, Emma has just got swallowed inside of the middle of the slide with her bottom entering inside first, I bet she is so frightened!"

Chapter Nine

Slide

Sharon sounded puzzled. "Where has Emma gone, I wonder, and with it being high up, I bet the sun drinks out of sunglasses!"

Leon smirked, sounding thunderstruck. "The slide is lifting into the air like it's as light as a feather!"

Sharon sounded overwhelmed. "Oh no, now the slide has lifted into the air, Emma must be trapped inside!"

Leon sounded worried. "How will Emma get out from inside of the slide?"

Sharon sounded panicked. "I guess that the slide is trying to kill people!"

Leon noticed. "Emma is falling through the air onto Ava, I wonder how Emma got out?"

Sharon announced. "Emma has got her lipstick knife in her hand, I bet she used that to cut her way out of the slide!"

Leon pointed. "Yes, I think you are correct, and look, Ava doesn't look very pleased, she has just announced that it feels like she has been run over again!"

Sharon sighed. "That's why Ava always looks in pain!"

Leon agreed. "Yes, it will be the injection bringing all of her pain back with a vengeance until it goes as it did back to that first week that she got run over!"

Sharon sounded sad. "Yes, it will be ten times worse for Ava now that Emma has landed on top of her!"

Leon gasped. "Emma is cuddling Ava!"

Sharon sounded cheerful. "Emma is thanking Ava for being her cushion and she is demanding that Ava must never go on the slide if it ever lowers to the ground!"

Leon sounded jolly. "Ava and Emma are cuddling each other; it's making me wonder if they are into each other!"

Sharon sounded flabbergasted. "Look, Ava and Emma are kissing each other romantically, I really wasn't expecting that, I was expecting a fight of some sort!"

Leon spat his drink out. "This is live television; Ava is playing with Emma's breasts!"

Sharon laughed. "This is better than a porn show!"

Leon moaned. "It's getting good and episode four is finishing, this is so disappointing and your top needs washing now!"

Sharon begged. "Please carry it on in real life instead and play with my breasts like Ava did, it looked so nice and raunchy!"

They walked upstairs and got onto the bed with Leon stripping Sharon's clothes. "I love playing with your warm soft breasts, they feel amazing, and your nipples feel lovely and smoothly hard!"

Sharon groaned. "I am really not sure who is enjoying it more, me or you!"

Leon sucked and licked Sharon's breasts. "This is much better than candy any day!"

Sharon groaned. "Please move downwards and lick my clit!"

Leon smiled. "Anything for you, my queen of my truncheon!"

Sharon shut her eyes. "I will strip you, then I can play with you as well!"

Leon stopped licking Sharon's clit. "I love it when you strip me, it gets me excited!"

Sharon sat on Leon's penis. "I will ride you for a little while!"

Leon announced. "I can't keep my sperm back because you turn me on so much; it is ejaculating inside of you right now!"

Sharon sighed. "I enjoyed that, and it felt so comforting, let's go to sleep so that we are fresh as a daisy tomorrow!"

They woke up and enjoyed the day going for a walk and then watched television with it getting to nine o 'clock with Leon speaking. "It feels like time has fast-forwarded because episode five is starting and the violins are playing a sweet tune; I wonder what is going to happen tonight!"

Sharon sounded surprised as episode five started. "Emma and Ava look comfy together giving each other a massage, Ava still looks in pain near her stomach area, someone is screaming really loudly, this sounds intriguing!"

Leon pointed at Joseph. "I am happy for Emma and Ava, look, Joseph is screaming, he isn't having much luck because he was in the middle of a rainstorm, and he also had his nose busted by Ava for landing on her, and he is now having a light shone into his eyes by a drone that has flown down from the sky, the drone has grabbed hold of Joseph around his waist trapping his arms so that he can't move!"

Joseph cried. "I feel trapped and scared!"

Sharon sounded anxious. "Oh my gosh, Joseph is being tortured with light being shone in his eyes, the red drone is lifting his eyelids, and this is stopping him from shutting his eyes, I wonder how long that will last, it could blind him and damage his eyes!"

Leon sounded fearful. "I think that Joseph will end up blind if that carries on because the drone is so vicious, I have never seen a drone like that before, it looks really scary, I am glad that I am this side of the screen!"

Sharon sounded disgusted. "I imagine the drone will have been made especially for this job!"

Leon sounded sympathetic. "I guess you are right, oh dear, his mouth looks like it's still in pain from when he first went into the jungle, I thought that would be better by now!"

Sharon pointed at Benjamin. "Benjamin's leg still looks painful the way that he is walking, I suppose if he broke his leg years ago it would have taken a while to heal back then, so it will take a while to get better now, and Benjamin's eyes are focused on a board hanging from a tree!"

Leon read the board. "It is another fact, it says that it is estimated that four billion trees are standing in the Amazon rainforest, and the trees influence rainfall cycles throughout South America by releasing twenty billion tonnes of water into the air daily, remarkably, a single large tree can release over one thousand litres of water over twenty-four hours and this can fill ten average-sized bathtubs!"

Sharon laughed. "That's unbelievable but true, and I am just thinking about the sad vampire, do you know what he had to cheer him up?"

Leon shouted. "I have got no idea of the answer and oh no, Drew is walking towards Benjamin, and Drew is giving him an evil look for looking in his bag earlier!"

Sharon sounded stressed. "B positive is the answer to my vampire joke and the red drone is very persistent at attacking Joseph with its suckers on his eyes; it is very intense with-it attracting Benjamin and Drew through Joseph's screams!"

Niall Orange and Sophie Ball discuss if they think Joseph will be able to see still.

Leon sounded fearful. "I think this television game is a bit brutal, don't you think?"

Sharon agreed. "At least it's keeping us wanting more, and Drew is trying to help Joseph to remove the drone by trying to pull the drones rubber suckers off Joseph's eyes unsuccessfully!"

Leon sounded stressed. "Benjamin is now trying to help Joseph by trying to bash the red drone with his hands away from Joseph's eyes!"

Chapter Ten

Squirrel Monkeys

Benjamin screeched. "Leave Joseph alone, you are hurting him!"

Sharon sounded surprised. "Finally, the drone has flown away high into the air, I presume that Benjamin must have frightened it away!"

Joseph shuffled over to Benjamin with his eyes shut and grabbed his hand, shaking it. "My eyelids hurt, but at least you saved me. Thank you, Benjamin, for your support!"

Leon sounded disappointed. "Episode five has just finished because the violins are playing!"

Sharon sounded a little sad turning the television off." We will have to wait for episode six to start tomorrow to find out what kicks off!"

Leon put his arm around Sharon. "We need to go to bed, I suppose I could kiss every part of your body!"

Sharon stripped off on the way upstairs. "Please kiss me from head to foot, Leon!"

Leon and Sharon lay on the bed naked, with Leon speaking. "Your body feels so soft, warm and tender, I love kissing your amazing body, Sharon!"

Sharon groaned. "That's better than a full English breakfast any day!"

Leon laughed. "I will make you a full English breakfast in the morning if you like!"

Sharon smiled. "Definitely, I will enjoy that as much as this!"

Leon kissed Sharon on her vagina's lips. "I am really enjoying licking your clit, it tastes so nice!"

Sharon groaned. "I am really enjoying you licking it!"

Leon moved upwards towards Sharon's breasts, speaking. "Your breasts are so firm, and your nipples feel amazing to suck!"

Sharon was breathing heavily, reaching for his penis. "Your penis is solid as a rock; I am desperate for your penis inside of me, please, fuck me silly!"

Leon teased Sharon. "I am moving in your clit a little to tease you!"

Sharon pushed her bottom upwards. "Put it all the way in, I need your sperm to fill my clit completely!"

Leon put his penis inside of Sharon. "Your clit is so wet, warm and inviting, I am feeling the urge to fill your walls with my warm sticky sperm!"

Sharon screamed. "I am so hot, give me every bit, I love the penetration of your love juices entering inside of me!"

Leon announced. "I am ejaculating inside of your tight clit now; it feels like a water slide with you being so wet with both of us spilling our juices in perfect sync together!"

Sharon suggested. "I think we should go to sleep and enjoy our day going to crazy golf and enjoy a walk tomorrow!"

Nine o 'clock soon arrived the next day with Leon sounding happy. "Finally, episode six is starting because the violins are playing! "

Sharon pointed at Amelia. "Amelia and Marie are getting attacked by a pair of squirrel monkeys, they look frightened!"

Leon pointed above Amelia's and Marie's heads. "Look, there is a massive bunch of bananas above their heads so the squirrel monkeys must be trying to take the food before Marie and Amelia get a chance to get it!"

Sharon sounded worried. "The squirrel monkeys are trying their best to get the bananas as they are dropping to the floor!"

Leon sounded shocked. "I can't believe that the bananas have dropped on top of Marie and Amelia's heads, I bet it hurt them because bananas would be heavy and sharp in a large bunch, that is my opinion!"

Sharon sounded relieved. "At least the squirrel monkeys have got their bananas now so they should leave Marie and Amelia alone, they look like they are full of cuts because they are randomly bleeding through their clothes in different places!"

Leon chuckled. "Do you know what you call a monkey with a banana in each ear?"

Sharon shrugged her shoulders. "I am sure that you will tell me!"

Leon sounded surprised. "Anything you like because they can't hear you and look, Amelia still looks in pain all over her body with her using her first aid kit to patch up her wounds, and it has announced that it's coming to the end of week one already, the people that have donated items for them to use are entering into the game tonight!"

Sharon could not help but read the large board hanging from a tree. "It says that one hundred and fifty to two hundred billion tons of carbon is stored in the Amazon rainforests and soils, and this is vital to fight the climate crisis and limit the rise in global temperatures!"

Leon sounded intrigued. "I didn't realise that the rainforest was so important!"

Sharon pointed. "Look, Marie and Amelia are trying to eat all of the bananas that they can, and they are stuffing as many as they can in their transparent rook sacks for later!"

Leon stared. "Marie is offering Amelia a chocolate bar!"

Sharon sounded distraught. "Brandon still looks upset because he's covered in ants from head to foot!"

Leon sounded disgusted. "There is a tea cosy that has fallen from the sky and a big bag full of individual packets of crisps has also fallen from the sky with messages attached to each bag!"

Sharon sounded surprised. "Brandon has used the tea cosy to remove the ants from his body, and he has just read a crisp packet, it says that he has got to play darts!"

Leon sounded confused. "How can Brandon play darts in the jungle?"

Sharon sounded puzzled. "I don't know, but a dart board has just appeared with random pieces of rubbish on it that he could win, and it says underneath that the booby prize is a coffin for him to dig himself out of!"

Leon sounded shocked. "Now he has won what it looks like a black rubbish bag!"

Sharon gasped. "Brandon has read that it would be his body bag if he loses!"

Leon sounded gobsmacked. "That's shocking and brutal, he has hit another prize, a load of confetti has just exploded out of the dartboard!"

Chapter Eleven

Cardboard Squares

Sharon shook a little. "This is creepy, Brandon has won a gun now, that's just encouraging him to shoot everyone so that he can win all of the money for himself!"

Leon sounded relieved. "The dart board has vanished, that was a waste of time!"

Sharon sounded miserable. "Niall Orange has just announced that episode six is finishing already. That is disappointing, even though I love the sound of the violins!"

Leon picked Sharon up and carried her upstairs. "I will cheer you up now that you are on the bed!"

Sharon sounded happy with every piece of clothing that was removed. "I love it when you strip me it's exciting, will you concentrate on my legs, I love it when you touch my legs gently, it turns me on so much!"

Leon smiled. "Your wish is granted, any part of you is so beautiful, especially your smile!"

Sharon sounded thankful. "I am so glad you are here in my life, sharing every precious moment with me!"

Leon sounded loved. "I am totally smitten with you. You make my stomach feel like butterflies when I am with you. I am sure that I could do cartwheels if I tried!"

Sharon laughed. "You would end up in the doctor's room if you did, I am sure, so don't bother, just carry on tickling my legs where you can relax instead of doing acrobatics activities!"

Leon muttered softly. "Am I teasing you enough with my warm, gentle and soft, long, fat, tickling fingers?"

Sharon smirked. "Oh yes, definitely, carry on!"

Leon sounded cheeky. "I couldn't resist it, I had to put my fingers inside of your warm clit and your body is so amazing, everything from your slim cute bottom to your eyes turns me on!"

Sharon sounded erotic. "Wow, you are so gentle and so special to me, matching me on the same wavelength as bacon and eggs!"

Leon laughed. "There you go again; you are talking about your cooked breakfast, once again!"

Sharon demanded. "Please put your penis inside of my clit and fuck me hard!"

Leon smiled. "I don't need to be asked twice; I am diving in!"

Sharon screamed with joy. "That's amazing, I can't control my orgasm, your rapid thrusts are tantalisingly amazing!"

Leon sounded sexually aroused. "That's better than when you sneeze with the feeling of my sperm intensifying like a trigger shooting inside of you!"

Sharon smiled. "You are always my number one guilty pleasure!"

Leon sounded desired. "I could do that again if I didn't feel sleepy, I think the endorphins are kicking in!"

Sharon whispered softly. "Good night then, we can go to the new dance class in Wakefield town hall if you like tomorrow, and then we can go to the Crumbs sandwich shop!"

Leon sounded exhilarated. "I am looking forward to tomorrow, I can't wait to learn how to dance with you, good night!"

Sharon and Leon sat down on the sofa after a long, busy fun day with Sharon holding Leon's hand. "You may as well sell your house, Leon, and come and live with me because I want you here all the time to keep me company in every way!"

Leon agreed. "I want to stay with you as well, I am glad that episode seven is starting with the violins playing a dramatic tune, someone may find the clock today!"

Sharon sounded exhilarated. "Maybe because they look exhausted, and Sophie Ball is saying how proud she is of the contestants keeping going in a terrible situation! "

Leon sounded optimistic. "I suppose they will be shattered and in pain, look, there's cardboard squares on the ground with some saying boom on and some have got drop written on others!"

Sharon sounded confused. "I don't like the sound of that, I wonder if that means that whoever plays the game will go boom and get blown into the air and die!"

Leon sounded a little sad. "I dread to think what drop means in this game, it could mean anything!"

Sharon nodded. "Both options sound as bad as each other!"

Leon gasped. "Oh no, Drew is walking towards the cardboard squares!"

Sharon sounded petrified. "I just felt a chill down my spine for Drew if he goes near it!"

Leon sounded horrified. "I thought that you had something on your face, and at least Drew is walking away, it looks like he has got some sense!"

Sharon pointed. "Oh no, look drones are pulling Drew towards the cardboard, making him stand on it and I can't feel anything on my face!"

Leon stared at the drone. "It's something called the look of worry and fright on your face and look Drew has got to answer a question that is written on a piece of paper that was laid on top of the cardboard square!"

Sharon sounded downhearted. "You are daft, you made me think that I had spilt something on my face, and I think that if he gets the answer wrong to the question, something extremely bad will happen to him!"

Leon sounded a little tense. "Don't keep us in suspense, please answer it correctly Drew!"

Sharon sounded positive. "He has just read the question out, I guess the answer is English people to which country drinks the most coffee!"

Leon sounded frightened. "Drew has said Finland; I hope that he is correct for his own sake to stay alive!"

Sharon sounded stressed. "I wonder if I was correct, or Drew was right?"

Chapter Twelve

Apple Throwing

Leon smiled. "Drew was correct. The answer is on the cardboard below his feet; it says Finland written in large black writing!"

Sharon gulped. "Look, there is a boom noise with what it looks like a large sparkler that has started to crackle, and it is now making a louder boom noise in front of his face!"

Leon sounded startled. "If that's what he has won, I don't know what the consolation prize would have been because the sparks could blind him!"

Sharon sounded troubled. "He could find out in a minute if he gets the next answer wrong what the loser's prize is, I don't think he will like it!"

Leon sounded upset. "There are another three cardboard squares to stand on, including the one he is standing on!"

Sharon sounded edgy. "It's asked Drew how many stars are on the Chinese flag, and I think that it is four stars!"

Leon sounded relieved. "It's five stars, I think!"

Sharon bit her nails, shouting. "It's five stars, you and Drew were correct!"

Leon smiled. "I am happy that he is getting the answers correct!"

Sharon sounded happier. "Drew is smashing it; I don't like the sparks because I know they will be hot!"

Leon sounded confused. "It has asked him what colour a polar bear's skin is, it is obviously white or skin coloured!"

Sharon agreed. "Drew thinks that it is skin colour as well the answer!"

Leon sounded gutted. "It says that it is black, and Drew has just dropped through the cardboard, I dread to think where he has gone!"

Sharon wiped a tear from her eye. "Drew is possibly dead!"

Leon sounded astounded. "The cardboard squares have sunk into the ground like a sponge and Ava is walking towards where Drew fell into the floor, I bet Drew is alive shouting for help!"

Sharon gasped. "Ava has got her ear to the ground listening; he could be in a snake pit or anything!"

Leon sounded staggered. "I can't believe what my eyes are seeing, Ava is stripping her clothes off, and it looks like she is being controlled because she is having a conversation with herself, by the way Niall Orange is talking, he thinks that Ava has lost the plot!"

Sharon scowled. "I really do think that she is either putting on a good act, or it's real like you said!"

Leon sounded positive. "I don't know what is controlling Ava, but the only thing I can say is that I think that she must be doing what someone says because she looks like she's in a world of her own with her staring in front of her and not taking any notice of what is going on around her, and Sophie Ball sounds concerned about Ava!"

Sharon sounded upset. "Oh no, it is the end of week one already with the violins playing!"

Leon sounded down." That is disappointing, we will have to find out what happens with Ava tomorrow!"

Sharon puckered her lips. "Please give me a kiss, Leon, that will make me feel better!"

Leon sounded horny. "Your lips turn me on, I feel like I need you to relieve me!"

Sharon smiled. "I am grabbing hold of your dick; I am loving massaging it up and down with my hands!"

Leon groaned. "I am enjoying it more, your hands feel magical, and your nipples are lovely and hard!"

Sharon begged. "Please suck my nipples, I feel so wet, and you are making me feel very aroused!"

Leon whispered. "I feel like I am going to explode like a volcano, I need to fill your clit with my dick now!"

Sharon wiped the sweat from her eyebrow. "You are making me feel so hot!"

Leon pushed his dick inside of Sharon's clit. "You are so wet you could cause an avalanche, but it feels so good!"

Sharon smiled. "You are making me even wetter; I feel sorry for the neighbours because they will need a boat soon!"

Leon announced. "I am ejaculating inside of you now!"

Sharon sounded relieved. "It was amazing, we can enjoy our day tomorrow at the Barnsley Metro Dome swimming pool!"

Leon sounded happy. "I can't believe that day one of week two is starting already, today has flown by with us having such a good time, and the people playing the violins are so talented!"

Sharon sounded excited. "Wow, look, Ava is still wondering around where Drew had disappeared!"

Leon gasped. "Amelia is walking towards Ava; I wonder what will happen!"

Sharon sounded horrified. "Ava looks like she is temporarily not in pain with her stomach as much, she is picking apples out of a large container and throwing the apples at Amelia like she is a human dart board!"

Leon sounded distraught. "Amelia has still got so much dried blood on her from the squirrel monkey attack, and she looks like she's crying!"

Sharon drank her beer. "I am glad I was not attacked by the squirrel monkey!"

Leon sounded surprised. "Amelia is shouting Brandon's name!"

Sharon sounded sad. "Amelia will trust Brandon because Brandon didn't shoot Amelia and if you remember, he then kissed her on week one and episode one and look, Amelia's foot looks sore, it looks like she is struggling to walk with her obviously being still in pain, Amelia probably needs a bit of comfort!"

Leon sounded distressed. "Joseph is picking the apples up from the floor and eating them that Ava has been throwing at Amelia!"

Sharon laughed. "At least Joseph is being resourceful, and he seems happy enough because he's got something to eat, he does look a little bit like he is struggling to eat slightly still with his mouth being slightly hurting by the look of it the way that he's chewing very slowly!"

Leon stared at Joseph. "It looks like Joseph has recovered from the drone shining the light into his eyes, but his nose still looks painful from

Ava busting his nose for landing on her, and his legs look muddy from the rainstorm!"

Sharon sounded shaken up. "It looks like Brandon isn't coming to help Amelia, he can't be in the area!"

Leon sounded disappointed. "No, and I bet those apples are hurting Amelia, I guess she will be full of bruises!"

Sharon sounded down in the dumps. "In my opinion, Amelia will be killed by the way the apples are hitting her because they are fast and hard

flowing through the air as they hit her!"

Chapter Thirteen

Piano Tune

Leon sounded shocked. "It says on a poster that is attached to a tree that Ava will only stop throwing apples at Amelia if Amelia can kill somebody or something!"

Sharon breathed heavily. "Oh no, Amelia is getting her bow and arrow from her rook sack ready for action!"

Leon gulped. "Joseph has run away, and Marie is walking towards Amelia!"

Niall Orange gets over-excited with all of the drama and chaos.

Sharon sounded tense. "Oh heck, Marie has got her scissors in her hand, and she is walking a little strange, it looks like she has still got her back pain!"

Leon sounded like he was in a tizzy. "Ava isn't stopping throwing apples at all; if anything, in my opinion,

I think that Ava is throwing the apples faster at Amelia!"

Sharon had a nervous giggle. "I think that Amelia is trying to stop herself from killing Marie by dragging herself away from Marie because Amelia is trying to run away the opposite way!"

Leon rubbed his arm. "I bet Amelia is running away because she must have enjoyed drinking the vodka and eating the chocolate with Marie the other day, and they tried to climb a tree together as well as surviving the banana attack between them!"

Sharon moved her feet around in a random movement. "Marie and Amelia will obviously get on well, and they have formed a bond, so they will not want to intentionally hurt each other!"

Leon sounded unimpressed. "Amelia must be trying to find someone else to kill, I am surprised that Amelia can see with all the apples hitting her, and I am just thinking, do you know why the apple pie went to the dentist?"

Sharon shrugged her shoulders. "I have got no idea?"

Leon answered. "Because the apple pie needed filling, and do you know what lives inside of an apple?"

Sharon had a nervous giggle, sounding concerned. "I don't know, maybe a seed and I hope that Brandon doesn't turn up because Marie attempted to smother Brandon with her sleeping bag, and Brandon stole Marie's food so there could be trouble ahead!"

Leon sat tight, smirking. "The answer is a bookworm, and Benjamin is walking towards Amelia now, in between the trees, if Amelia notices Benjamin, I am sure that Amelia will kill Benjamin!"

Sharon sounded astonished with a cheesy grin. "That is the first time that we have seen Benjamin for a while, I bet Benjamin has been hiding away from Drew with him trying to touch Benjamin's bag!"

Leon sounded blunt to the point. "Benjamin will have been keeping away from the haunted house with a knife nearly hitting him as well as his bad leg, giving him agony I guess!"

Sharon pointed. "Look, Amelia has just shot her arrow at Benjamin, oh dear, I wouldn't like to be in his shoes at the moment because there's no chance of any kind of prescription coming their way!"

Benjamin struggled to speak. "I feel like I am in deep danger, and I am about to die!"

Leon sounded tense. "Wow, Benjamin is about to die with no help around, and Niall Orange is being over dramatic, saying that there will be a death!"

Sharon sounded shocked." Oh, what a shocker, Benjamin has just bent down to pick up some matches that he had dropped on the floor!"

Leon sounded frightened. "Oh, my goodness, the arrow has hit a Jaguar instead that was about to bite Benjamin, I think that he was very lucky bending down at the correct moment so that he wasn't killed!"

Sharon smirked. "At least on the bright side they have got something to eat if they cook it and, as you said, Benjamin has been lucky to still be alive and kicking!"

Leon sounded relieved. "Ava has finally stopped throwing apples at Amelia now that Amelia has killed the

Jaguar, I don't know what Amelia will use from her first aid kit, she will have nothing left soon at the rate she is going with her injuries!"

Sharon sounded sad. "Look at Amelia's bruised body, it looks so painful!"

Leon sounded comforted. "Yeah, Amelia does look to be in pain the way she is gently touching herself and Ava looks confused!"

Sharon had a disappointing look. "I guess that Ava was definitely controlled somehow by a secret hypnotist hiding near her!"

Leon agreed. "Yeah, I am positive that the game has taken control of her, I am happy for Amelia because her ordeal is finally over!"

Sharon sounded devastated. "Oh no, day one of week two has finished, this is making me feel sad because the violins are playing again!"

Leon sounded mushy. "Let's go into the garden and look at the stars because looking up at the sky is so precious, and it makes us feel alive with gladness that we can have the beauty of vision!"

Sharon smiled. "That would be a change from going to bed straight away because the weather is warm for a change, and the summerhouse sofa looks invitingly comfortable!"

Leon looked up at the sky with star-gazed eyes. "The moon above the trees looks so nice and the stars are shining so bright, this feels so romantic, let's enjoy sexy play in the garden under the stars!"

Sharon laid on the grass. "I love being able to see the stars as well as your gorgeous, amazing body, but this grass is a little bit cool!"

Leon sounded a little nervous. "I just hope that the neighbours aren't watching us!"

Sharon laughed. "I doubt that they will be at this time of night, and I think that it makes it more exciting the thought of us being watched, don't you agree, and other people viewing our fun could turn us on even more?"

Leon stripped Sharon's clothes while Sharon stripped Leon with Sharon mentioning. "The neighbours may enjoy rolling around the grass with us and they may have just finished watching the pain game as well!"

Sharon led the way into the summerhouse. "That's true, and it is a little bit comfier in here with us being able to relax on the sofa, I have left the door open wide Just in case my neighbours want to join us!"

Leon got comfortable. "I am loving sucking your nipples they taste better than toffee!"

Sharon started to suck Leon's nipples and then moved downwards to his dick. "This is nice, but I think that you are going to have to fill my clit soon!"

A neighbour opened their upstairs window, shouting. "Go for it, you two, I can see that you both intensely enjoyed your nipples being sucked!"

Leon shouted back to the neighbour. "I intend to, don't worry!"

Chapter Fourteen

Orange Button

Sharon demanded Leon to fill her clit. "Please fill me with your love juices because I am yearning for you!"

Leon got on top, massaging Sharon's breasts with his soft hands. "I am thrusting inside of you with my penis; it feels so amazing!"

Sharon lifted her bottom up towards Leon's warm body with her speaking. "I can't control my orgasm; you are so hard!"

Leon groaned. "I am orgasming myself right now!"

Sharon and Leon lay side by side for a few minutes with Sharon speaking. "The stars are as amazing as you are, let's go to bed and enjoy our day tomorrow!"

Leon and Sharon went to bed, they then went ice skating and enjoyed food out until nine pm the next day.

Leon sounded shocked that day two of week two was about to start. "Come and sit with me Sharon because the game is about to start because the violins are playing a cute tune!"

Sharon sounded intrigued. "I wonder how it's going in the jungle, oh wow, there was a snippet of what it looked like a gold clock then, did you see it?"

Leon sounded unimpressed. "Maybe, look, Emma has got a piano shirt on, it says on the keys on her shirt that she needs to play a tune on the piano that is hidden among the trees!"

Sharon had a worried tone of voice. "I dread to think what will happen if Emma doesn't find the piano, and the musical part of a snake is the scales!"

Leon laughed. "A piano will be too big for her not to find and the best way to play music on your head is through a headband!"

Sharon tittered, sounding distraught. "Wow, the piano is hanging high up in mid-air with a wire connecting to a tree at either side, I dread to think how Emma is going to get up there!"

Leon sounded alarmed. "There is no safety gear for Emma to use, she will be the second person to die because Drew hasn't appeared back yet from the floor, and someone must have risked their life to get the piano up there, and Sophie Ball looks upset with what could happen!"

Sharon scratched her neck. "Knowing the people in charge of this game, it will have been a poor person who will not be missed!"

Leon wiped a tear from his eye. "Most probably, yes!"

Sharon sounded in awe. "Look, Emma is climbing the tree, and she has slipped off the branches many times already, how is she going to walk on that wire and play the piano without her falling to the ground with a bang and broken bones, or even death, and look, Niall Orange looks like he is going to cry?"

Emma wiped a tear from her eye. "I really don't want to do this, but I have got to do it!"

Leon gasped. "As Emma is getting further up the tree, it is like something or someone is sending her some help because extra branches are growing from the tree for her to use, and the wire is starting to turn into a walkway with nothing to hold on to that will stop her from falling to her gruesome death!"

Sharon put her hands over her eyes. "I can't watch; Emma is about to walk on the walkway!"

Leon spoke with gritted teeth. "Emma is slowly walking towards the piano, the walkway is moving as she walks from side to side, making it even more difficult for her!"

Sharon bit her nail. "Emma has finally made it, she is playing a tune on the piano, it says that she has got immunity from getting killed for the night on the piano lid and I think that pianists are like lightning because they rarely strike the same key twice!"

Emma sounded proud. "I am happy that I have achieved something that was almost impossible to do!"

Leon sounded pleased, smiling. "I am pleased for Emma, and I liked your little piano joke, and I wonder if she will have to get herself back down to the ground from up there at the top of the trees!"

Sharon sounded gobsmacked. "No, Emma is lucky because she is about to jump into a floating large hammock that is dropping from the sky with a helicopter above the hammock that is dangling down from the sky!"

Leon put his hands on either side of his face, sounding relieved. "I am happy for Emma; I wonder how she will stay safe!"

Sharon's eyes lit up brightly. "A doorway has opened up in the floor for Emma to walk into with her walking inside now that she's on the ground!"

Leon sounded in a good mood. "Emma has got food and a bed to sleep in, that's good, it's like her own private safe room!"

Sharon sounded erratic. "It's small but safe underground away from danger, but look, Drew is at the other side of the glass to Emma trapped in the darkroom!"

Leon gasped. "Amelia is banging on the glass to get Drew's attention with her having no response from him, and it says on the glass that the only way for Drew to get out is for someone to find the orange button, and if the orange button is not found and pressed Drew will die!"

Sharon caught her breath. "That's brutal, nobody will want to help Drew in the darkroom because they all want to win, Amelia has shut her safe room door until tomorrow, and it's getting a little tiny bit closer to week two ending, so the pressure is on for them all!"

Leon sounded skittish. "Wow, Benjamin is back, look, a person from the public has sent a bag full of nothing with a hole in the bottom of the bag that has just landed on the floor in front of Benjamin's feet, and Benjamin has put the bag inside of his transparent ruck sack, and their red coats are so bright!"

Sharon pointed out. "It's like the pain game camera is following Benjamin around!"

Leon screamed. "Look, the orange button that is needed to release Drew from the darkroom is next to where Benjamin is walking!"

Sharon sounded shocked. "Benjamin is going to pick the orange button up; I can't believe that Niall Orange is screaming for Benjamin to pick the button up!"

Leon sounded puzzled. "Benjamin has picked it up from the ground, and just looked at it with a puzzled look, and he has thrown it back onto the floor like a piece of rubbish because he doesn't know what it does!"

Chapter Fifteen

Blindfold, Whip, Handcuff

Sharon sounded disappointed. "Benjamin is walking towards Joseph, and it looks like Drew is still stuck underground!"

Leon sounded in awe. "Joseph has just invited Benjamin into his tent because it's so hot to have a breather away from the sun, it's like the sun stays in the sky longer there, Sophie

Ball is mentioning how glad she is that she is not in the jungle!"

Sharon mentioned. "At least the tent is open so that Benjamin can get away from Joseph if he needs to if he fears for his life!"

Leon sounded happy. "At least Benjamin and Joseph are being friendly with each other instead of being bitter towards one another and I bet that it is hot inside of the tent!"

Sharon sounded upset. "Another day is over; I think that it is about to end for tonight because the violins are starting to play!"

Leon complained. "Well, we will have to wait until tomorrow to see if Benjamin and Joseph are still talking!"

Sharon turned off the television and started smooching around Leon. "That's the end of day two of week two!"

Leon started to sing, trying to stay in the rhythm of the violins. "You are the best, you are as sweet as a cake sits on a plate! "

Sharon smiled. "I have turned the television off, and I think you are as cute as a kitten!"

Leon picked Sharon up. "I am carrying you upstairs, then I will slowly strip you when I have given you my special gift!"

Sharon sounded excited. "Ooh, that is thoughtful of you, what have you got me?"

Leon smiled. "You will have to open it to find out! "

Sharon ripped open the paper. "Wow, a whip, a blindfold and a pair of handcuffs and at the bottom of it all is a beautiful necklace with a gold heart pendant on it, I am one of the luckiest ladies alive to have you!"

Leon sounded joyful. "I am so pleased you like your gifts; I will put your necklace on, and we can then play with our new toys!"

Sharon kissed Leon with passion. "The necklace looks so pretty on my neck, we could use the blindfold now, what do you suggest?"

Leon's eyes lit up. "You don't need the necklace to make you look any more gorgeous than you already are, your eyes sparkle like a million stars in the sky!"

Sharon sounded loved. "I really do think that we make a great lovers team!"

Leon sounded in love. "I love every bit of you from deep in my heart!"

Sharon smiled. "I think our life is changing forever for the better!"

Leon suggested. "Now that I have put your blindfold over your eyes, you could thank me by finding my dick with your mouth and suck it without using your hands!"

Sharon laughed. "Course I will, this sounds like fun, now that we are naked, I have put my blindfold on, it reminds me of our own crazy version of Pin the Tail on the Donkey!"

Leon shook with laughing. "I can tell that you really can't see at all because you are in the wrong place, that's as far as my belly button that you have got!"

Sharon finally found Leon's dick. "Wow, your cock is so fat, smooth, hard, warm and long, it feels like I am sucking a warm, comforting lollipop!"

Leon sexually groaned. "This feels amazing, I feel so fulfilled with erotic pleasure!"

Sharon demanded. "Please lick my clit at the same time!"

Leon sounded refreshed. "I will fill your clit with my cock!"

Sharon sounded aroused. "I am loving this; you are making me feel so hot and sexually aroused!"

Leon apologised. "I am sorry, but I can't keep my love juices back from you any longer, I will have to fill your clit, I love your toned body, just looking at you makes me hot under the collar!"

Leon ejaculated inside of Sharon.

Sharon screamed. "That was so nice with the penetrations of your sperm entering inside of my clit!"

Leon suggested. "Let's go to the beach in Scarborough for the day tomorrow!"

Sharon nodded yes. "Let's get a good night's sleep first, I can't wait for tomorrow!"

Leon and Sharon went to Scarborough for the day, Leon

sounded happy as they got back home. "I loved us holding hands, walking along the beach the most and watching the sea lap up, it felt magical!"

Sharon reminisced. "The strawberry ice cream was really nice; the most important bit of this wonderful day is about to start!"

Leon sounded ecstatic. "Yes, day three of week two is starting and the violins are playing smoothly with a little sharpness in between!"

Sharon listened. "I think that the music has got an excellent fast beat, and the rhythm of the music is upbeat!"

Leon sounded a little staggered, pointing. "Look, Amelia must be out of her private safe room!"

Sharon sounded comforted. "Amelia looks like she is glowing in the face with energy and enthusiasm, with her enjoying a good night's sleep!"

Leon gulped. "Amelia is telling Benjamin and Joseph about Drew being in a darkened room and they need to find the orange button that needs pressing for Drew to survive!"

Sharon sounded unsettled. "Amelia is boasting to Benjamin and Joseph how safe she felt last night in her private safe room!"

Leon sounded cautious. "How odd, stepping stones and a small stream has appeared in between the trees, this looks dodgy, and Niall Orange is blowing everything out of proportion, as usual; he is very presumable guessing what will happen next!"

Sharon pointed out a handwritten note that had blown into the tent. "Look, it says that Benjamin and Joseph need to get to the other side of the stream without falling because if one of them falls in, they are both in trouble and Amelia is advising them not to do it!"

Chapter Sixteen

Water

Leon sounded baffled. "This game gets stranger, and Joseph has just read the note out saying that if they fall from the stepping stones, they will swap places with Drew underground in the darkroom and if they do reach the other side without falling into the water, Joseph and Benjamin will spend the night in the safe room where Amelia had slept the night!"

Sharon sounded scared. "Frighteningly, Joseph has started to walk over the stepping stones and Benjamin is just walking behind Joseph!"

Joseph mentioned to Benjamin. "We have got to walk slowly so that we have less chance of falling into the water!"

Benjamin walked slowly. "I do not intend to fall into the water because it will probably be cold with the sun beaming down, making us very warm, of course, we need to watch our step!"

Leon sounded gutted. "Look, Joseph has fallen into the water, at least the water will cool him down and he is unlucky with him not getting out as easily as he fell in with the shock of the cold water taking his breath away!"

Sharon cried. "A pair of water-shaped hands have formed from the water pulling Benjamin into the water with a very large splash, it looks like a circular tunnel has opened up in the water where they fell with them swirling into the middle of the choppy swirl!"

Leon sounded thunderstruck. "Wow, I thought the orange button had to be pressed for Drew to be released from his darkened room!"

Sharon guessed. "It must also work if someone swaps places with you!"

Leon sounded worried. "It looks like we won't see Joseph and Benjamin again for a while because they will be stuck in the darkroom now!"

Sharon stared at a large board. "It says that every minute an area roughly the size of five football pitches is cut down like it isn't important!"

Leon's eyes widened. "That is interesting information!"

Sharon stared. "Yes, it is, look, Drew is walking around looking a little dazed!"

Drew whispered to himself. "That was so stressful getting catapulted out of the darkroom!"

Leon guessed. "Drew will be confused because he's gone from a darkened room to bright, blinding sunshine!"

Sharon agreed. "Amelia is wandering around as well, and she has just started to fish for something to eat!"

Leon pointed. "Look, Brandon is getting covered in strawberries and not just a few, he will be struggling to breathe soon if he doesn't get away and all Sophie Ball can do is comment on how nice and sweet the strawberries look!"

Sharon sounded serious. "This is snow joke, a snowball maker that clamps together to make snowballs has fallen from the sky near to Brandon, he needs to use it to catapult the strawberries away from him or eat them, he is screaming for help with none on the way!"

Leon sounded anxious. "Someone will start eating the strawberries and find Brandon in the middle of them very soon most probably giving them an enormous shock of their life that they will least expect, and ice-cream makers learnt how to make ice-cream at sundae school!"

Sharon smiled, expressing her view. "I think Brandon is clever because he's shining his torch upwards, I guess the reason for this is so anyone that walks towards him will notice the light signal if it shines bright enough and they may help him get out of the strawberries if they want to!"

Leon raised his eyebrows, sounding concerned. "I think that Brandon is too wedged inside of the strawberries to use the snowball maker to flick them away from him and I am just thinking, I bet strawberries turn red because they watched the salad dressing!"

Sharon sniggered, sounding positive. "You are possibly correct, and at least it isn't ants crawling all over Brandon like on an earlier episode, that was just yucky!"

Leon sounded a little sad. "The strawberries have drowned Brandon completely; there's no sign of him at all and he has dropped silent!"

Sharon sounded hopeful. "Emma and Ava have walked near to Brandon, at least they have started to eat the strawberries, so there's a slight hope for Brandon to survive, I can't believe that the strawberries are still coming down as heavy making an even bigger pile of them!"

Leon sounded disappointed. "Emma and Ava are more interested in eating the strawberries and touching one another, and Niall Orange sounds like he is getting turned on looking at two ladies touching each other!"

Sharon sounded gobsmacked, fluttering her eyebrows. "Emma and Ava are stripping each others' clothes and sucking each others' breasts in between kissing each other!"

Leon's eyes were glued to the television. "Yes, I can see for myself, all I can say is that they must like one another because an audience watching them doesn't phase them!"

Sharon held her interest. "Emma and Ava are kissing each other's naked bodies; I really do think that they need to get dressed in case anybody comes along that feels like killing them!"

Leon's mouth was a jar. "They are licking each others' clits now!"

Sharon guessed. "If Emma and Ava get out alive, I am sure that they will keep in touch, they are definitely keeping us entertained!"

Leon licked his lips. "Wow, a chain saw has appeared from the sky with a note saying that Emma, Ava or anyone needs to make a useful item out of wood to release Brandon!"

Sharon stared at the television. "Emma is pointing at the slightest glimpse of the torchlight coming from Brandon that is buried under the beautiful Rosey red strawberries!"

Leon sounded disappointed. "Emma and Ava are getting into Ava's pop-up tent; I don't think that they are interested in making anything to help Brandon leave the strawberries and Emma is talking about the slide earlier, saying how frightened she and Amelia were!"

Sharon sounded scared. "Marie has appeared, and she has taken the chain saw, I dread to think what she is going to do with it!"

Leon sounded flabbergasted. "I can't believe how high the pile of strawberries is now, and it looks like Marie is filling her belly with the red fresh juicy strawberries before she goes!"

Chapter Seventeen

Sword

Sharon noticed. "Marie still looks in pain with her back!"

Leon mentioned. "The pain can't be bothering Marie that much with her picking up a heavy chainsaw!"

Sharon sounded surprised. "Marie is reading the note, and she looks puzzled, she has started to carve some trees up using the chainsaw, I wonder what she is making!"

Leon shrugged his shoulders. "I guess that she is making a weapon of some sort!"

Sharon agreed. "Yes, I guess that she is making some sort of sword with it being thin and long so that she can use it if she needs to later!"

Leon looked Marie up and down. "Marie looks as stocky as she was when she first entered into the jungle!"

Sharon agreed. "I agree, and I have never seen anybody trying to finish making a sword using a pair of scissors before!"

Leon laughed. "There is a first for everything, and that's the sharpest item that Marie had in her transparent rook sack!"

Sharon screeched. "Wow, look, the strawberries have finally finished falling on top of Brandon now that an item has been made, and Marie has dived into the strawberries like it's a swimming pool!"

Leon laughed. "Marie is swimming through the middle of them, kicking strawberries everywhere!"

Sharon smiled. "At least Marie is enjoying herself for a change!"

Niall Orange and Sophie Ball discuss how nice and tasty the strawberries look.

Leon sounded relieved. "Brandon's head is showing now that Marie has disturbed the strawberries, and I am just thinking, do you know what is red and goes up and down?"

Sharon chuckled. "I am not sure, maybe Father Christmas?"

Leon smiled. "A strawberry in an elevator!"

Sharon gave a slight giggle, sounding astonished. "Emma and Ava have left Ava's tent fully dressed; they look puzzled seeing Brandon stuck under the strawberries and Marie looks shocked to see Brandon!"

Leon sounded startled. "Look, the orange button that will release Joseph and Benjamin from the darkroom is just over there not far from the strawberries, but nobody has noticed it, and they don't know what it does!"

Sharon sounded upset. "It's a shame that they don't know what the orange button does, and I can't believe that Brandon is still alive, he looks exhausted and short of breath!"

Leon laughed. "I can't imagine how Brandon is feeling, and I can't understand how he has survived through his suffocating ordeal!"

Sharon nodded. "Brandon is struggling to catch his breath talking, but he is saying that the snowball maker helped him to survive with the mould being rounded outwards giving him a bit of room away from the strawberries, but he says that his head and body hurts from being crushed and compressed!"

Leon moaned. "I can't believe day two of week two is over already with the violins playing so elegantly smooth, I can't wait for tomorrow night already to see if Joseph and Benjamin are released from the darkroom, and we haven't seen any sign of the gold clock again!"

Sharon sounded like a balloon with no air inside. "Me too, I have turned the television off and it's so different to anything I have ever watched before in an interesting way keeping us hooked to the screen to find out what will happen next, and other new facts we can learn, I really do think this game is cruel, crazy, addictive and dangerous, I would definitely want out by now if I was in the game!"

Leon sounded positive. "At least it's on again tomorrow, give me your feet and I will give you a foot rub or massage or whatever you want to call it these days to cheer you up a bit!"

Sharon lifted her feet onto Leon's knees on the sofa. "Oh, that's lovely, that is making me feel better and more comfortable and relaxed already, Leon!"

Leon worked his way up Sharon's legs, using his fingertips. "That feels amazing Leon, your fingers feel so tenderly warm and soft!"

Sharon groaned. "You are making me feel so turned on, it's the best feeling in the world, I really don't know what I would do without you!"

Leon carried on higher up Sharon's body massaging. "Your breasts are lovely and smooth; I think that my dick would fit nicely between your soft and warm breasts, and I don't know what I would do without you either!"

Sharon moved her long hair to one side. "Put your knob between my breasts and rub it up and down, that will feel like an amazing tactile sensation, you make me feel so alive!"

Leon sounded engrossed. "This feels lovely and erotic; it's making me want to spurt all over your neck to give you an extra pearl necklace if that's okay with you?"

Sharon clasped her breasts together tightly, making a tight tunnel for his penis to move in and out of. "I am enjoying it as well!"

Leon had sweat running down his brow. "It's a good job because I am shooting my warm baby juices all over you now!"

Sharon laughed. "I have never seen as much creamy sperm, I had better get in the shower before we go to sleep, are you going to wash me?"

Leon sounded grateful. "I never thought that you would ask, course I will wash you, I love you so much, you feel like a gift that I am very happy that I had opened with very pleasing results!"

Sharon sounded delighted. "Your hands are so soft and as smooth as silk, and I couldn't think of a better person to be with!"

Leon stepped into the shower. "I thought I would get in with you, let's enjoy sex in the shower because I am getting turned on again!"

Sharon agreed. "Pick me up and make love to me again if you like, of course, that will make me happy!"

Leon put his penis inside of Sharon. "You are such a delight; I love the feel of your warm, welcoming and tight clit!"

Sharon shut her eyes, enjoying every thrust. "You are about to ejaculate again, aren't you?"

Leon groaned, moaning with pleasure. "Oh yeah, I love ejaculating inside of you, it's the best thing ever, it's a bit like releasing fireworks!"

Sharon smiled. "I love the feeling of it penetrating inside of me!"

Leon put Sharon down, they dried each other then laid on the bed with Leon speaking gently. "I love stroking your hair, it's so soft!"

Chapter Eighteen

Burnt Trees

Sharon and Leon fell asleep holding each others' bodies.

Sharon and Leon woke up, with Sharon suggesting. "Let's go to the beach and hire a jet ski for the day. What do you think?"

Leon sounded cheerful. "Oh, why not? We only live once, and this would be so good and a change from our usual day-to-day activities. Unfortunately, we have got to go back to work soon!"

They enjoyed their day on jet skis with a takeaway for tea while relaxing on the couch with Sharon sounding happy. "I am so pleased that day three of week two has started with the violins playing dramatically loud, it is making my emotions run high inside!"

Leon sounded emotional. "Me too, look, Drew is back, he has just picked a torch up from the ground, he can't put it down because it won't release from his hand as he opened them just then!"

Sharon sounded puzzled. "I don't know why the torch will not eject from Drew's hand!"

Leon's eyes lit up. "Oh, no, Drew's torch has started to produce flames, they are leaving the sides of the torch face, I bet he had triggered the flames to start with when he picked the torch up from the floor!"

Sharon gazed at the trees around Drew. "That's so dangerous, a fire isn't good in the middle of an extra-large jungle full of trees because they could all get killed with nobody getting the money!"

Leon shouted. "Yes, after all, the money is the aim of the game and Amelia is shouting at Drew; she is demanding that he has got to put the torch fire out before everything goes up in flames!"

Sharon sounded upset. "Yes, it is not a good situation!"

Leon smirked. "On the upside, at least Amelia has got a first aid kit to sort herself out if she gets burnt!"

Sharon sounded shocked. "Wow, Amelia has used her knife to cut the top of the torch off, but it's grown back to as it originally was, I don't know how that could happen, it must be some kind of magic or someone changing it somehow without Drew noticing!"

Leon agreed. "I couldn't believe that happened myself as well, I am surprised that they are all alive!"

Sharon gulped. "Drew has dropped the fire torch onto the floor; it's going to set the jungle and all of them on fire!"

Leon blinked as a tear rolled down his cheek. "It's too late, the jungle is on fire, and the smoke looks overwhelming!"

Sharon sounded devastated. "This is the end of the game, I guess!"

Leon sounded upset. "Drew and Amelia are running away from the fire, at least!"

Sharon sounded concerned. "A slide made of ice has appeared high above the flames, nobody will get on that because it will melt with the heat!"

Leon pointed. "Look, there is a note saying if someone gets onto the slide before it's been melted away by the flames below it, all of the flames will be put out by water drones!"

Sharon sounded astonished. "I don't know how they made the ice slide so fast, and I dread to imagine who would be brave enough to use it!"

Leon sounded astounded. "Emma has appeared, she is looking at the slide, mentioning how lovely, icy, refreshing, cooling, and great it looks away from the flames, and I am just thinking about the fire that went to school to get brighter!"

Sharon rolled her eyes, sounding a little frightened. "The slide is starting to melt already with it dripping to the ground fast and the ice is definitely getting thinner by the second!"

Leon sounded devastated. "Emma is climbing up the steps, and she is now sitting on the slide; I hope that she doesn't fall through the ice slide before she gets to the end!"

Sharon screamed. "Emma's bottom is stuck in the slide near to the end, she is trying to get onto the solid bit of the ice slide so that she can carry on!"

Leon gasped. "Emma is getting back onto the slide properly; I think she has saved the day because drones are finally putting the flames out!"

Sharon smiled. "I am pleased that the fire is slowly going out, and the ice slide has completely gone now with just a puddle left on the ground, you would never know that it had ever existed!"

Leon sounded preserved. "All of the trees are burnt black and steaming, but at least thankfully, the flames are out now!"

Sharon pointed. "Look, the orange button is on the floor by the burnt trees, I hope that someone picks it up and presses it to release Joseph and Benjamin before they die!"

Leon stared. "Emma has walked away, and Ava is walking towards the orange button!"

Sharon sounded disappointed. "Ava is standing looking down at the orange button, she needs to pick it up, it looks a little bit fire-damaged with it having black over the orange colour, but I am sure that it will be cool enough to pick it up without it burning her fingers!"

Leon sounded overwhelmed. "Ava is bending over looking at the button!"

Ava speaks to herself. "That button looks interesting; I wonder what it does?"

Sharon sounded excited. "Ava has picked the orange button-up, and she is looking at it strangely!"

Leon sounded panicked. "Ava is about to throw the orange button onto the floor, oh wait a minute, her hand is hovering over the orange button, I think that she's going to press the button to see what it does, or she will just try to clean it and press it by mistake, I guess!"

Sharon sounded relieved. "Ava has pressed the orange button, and Joseph and Benjamin have been catapulted into the air, Niall Orange is covering his face because it's getting a bit too intense for him, or that is my opinion by the petrified look on his face!"

Leon gulped. "I think that Joseph has landed not far from Ava, and I am not sure where Benjamin has landed, this injury will put them back even more and did you notice that Ava has put the orange button in her transparent rook sack?"

Chapter Nineteen

Springy Floor Ejects

Sharon pointed. "Ava is walking over to Joseph; they are discussing how cruel the game is with it hurting them even more than the pain accelerator injection that they received walking into the jungle and I am just thinking, my friend told me the other day that a person that they know, they work at a catapult factory as a manager, and they got the sack for firing people from the catapult factory building!"

Leon laughed, sounding interested. "Joseph is explaining to Ava that the dark roomed roof had opened up, then the floor turned into a springy floor ejecting them into the air with no warning what was about to happen to them!"

Sharon stared at a large board. "That's odd them ejecting into the air and it is sad because it says that seventeen per cent of the rainforest has been lost already, with it being equivalent to the size of France!"

Leon nodded. "Wow, that's a lot of rainforests that has gone already and it's an interesting fact to know!"

Sharon sounded doubtful. "I don't think that we will see the total end of the rainforest, I feel sorry for the future generations to live their lives!"

Leon sounded gutted. "Oh no, day three of week two has finished!"

Sharon gazed at Leon speaking. "Let's go to the shop and buy every different wine on the shelf so that we can do some wine tasting to see which ones we prefer out of all of them!"

Leon agreed, putting his shoes on. "This activity can go into tomorrow because it sounds like fun to me!"

They sat down on the sofa and tasted every wine, they then went to the local fayre for the afternoon enjoying many activities like hook a duck, as they got back from the fayre, they started to enjoy the rest of the wine together with Sharon speaking. "Come on, let's get fruity together to match the wine that we are drinking, I wish that we could have won a bottle of wine instead of a teddy!"

Leon asked Sharon. "I know a bottle of wine would have been good, but no, we had no such luck, and will you please massage my cock!"

Sharon sounded happy. "Of course I will, please, put some candy floss on my breasts and then lick it off!"

Leon laughed. "Okay, I can't wait to lick your breasts and eat the candy floss!"

Sharon sounded ecstatic. "This is great, your tongue is ticklish on my breasts, it's turning me on so much, it feels lovely and warm, and it is tantalisingly amazing giving me butterflies in my stomach, you make me feel super erotically turned on with my heart beating ten to the dozen!"

Leon glanced his eyes upwards towards Sharon's. "I am moving downwards, I am loving licking your clit, it tastes like nectar from a bee!"

Sharon begged. "Please fill my clit, I really do need you to fill my clit with your penis!"

Leon smiled. "I will definitely oblige to that request; I can't move in and out much faster than I am, I am so hot and bothered, but I am not bothered!"

Sharon sounded appreciated. "It feels so slippy down there, I could provide enough wetness to keep a water slide going!"

Leon laughed. "I am keeping my cock inside, I love your clit being so wet, I am ejaculating now, and the best thing is, it's nine pm and day four of week two is about to start!"

Sharon turned the television on. "Oh, the violins are playing calmly, look, Marie has got a drone chasing her with a chainsaw attached to the top of it with the chain moving so fast, and the noise from it is deafeningly loud!

Leon gulped. "Yeah, and Marie sounds so scared, I would be on the other side of the jungle by now if that was happening to me!"

Sharon sounded captivated. "They must have planned all of this to happen in advance, I bet they weren't expecting all of this to happen to them!"

Leon sounded petrified. "Marie is running around like a headless chicken trying not to get cut into pieces, I feel frightened for her!"

Sharon screamed. "Oh no, the chainsaw drone has just caught Marie's arm, err, there is blood dripping onto the ground, she needs to stop it from hurting her further!"

Leon gasped. "Marie is starting to climb a tree, but it will make no difference because the chainsaw drone is cutting the tree down that she has climbed up!"

Sharon sounded shocked. "Oh no, the tree is falling down, and Marie is about to fall out of the tree, I think that Marie is in deep trouble!"

Leon sounded sad. "I don't think her pen, paper, tarpaulin, scissors, a sleeping bag or a pan will help Marie one bit, all I can say is that she needs a miracle!"

Sharon had a tear rolling down her cheek. "Marie will not be able to run with her being a bit stocky, she has had it, she will bleed to death, and she will be cut up into tiny bits like a piece of soft cheese!"

Leon sounded surprised. "Benjamin has appeared, the chainsaw is chasing Benjamin now because he distracted the drone his way by shouting at it to leave them all alone, it's a good job because Marie looks white as a ghost in the face like she isn't very well, I guess her arm really hurts and she has lost a lot of blood!"

Sharon sounded surprised. "I am super shocked that Benjamin can even walk after being catapulted into the air and his leg still looks painful as he walks from the injection that he received as he walked into the jungle, inflicting the pain on purpose!"

Leon sounded gullible. "They will get away, I am sure!"

Sharon coughed. "I don't think Marie and Benjamin will get away from the chainsaw drone, this is a frightening situation that they are in!"

Leon sounded down. "Benjamin is distracting the chainsaw drone so that it stops attacking her, it is now leaving Marie, that's kind of him, I heard that there is a new chainsaw available soon and it is cutting technology!"

Sharon chuckled a little sounding shocked. "Benjamin has just had his leg caught by the chainsaw drone, and there are two bloody trails on the floor now going in different directions for the chainsaw drone to follow around!"

Leon sounded negative. "Benjamin will be caught in a minute, he needs to stop bleeding so that the drone can't follow the blood flow trail, I am glad that Marie has vanished, she must be in so much pain!"

Sharon sounded happier. "Ava is watching Benjamin from a distance, she is holding the orange button in her hand, it said at the beginning that the orange button could help or hinder, I wonder if that will help Benjamin if he gets the orange button off Ava?"

Chapter Twenty

Trail Of Blood

Leon sighed. "Ava is not going to go near to Benjamin, and I don't think Benjamin has noticed Ava!"

Sharon sounded concerned. "Benjamin is about to die because his bottom is going to be missing in a minute!"

Leon smirked. "Luckily, the chainsaw drone must be having some kind of battery problem because its power has cut off as it was starting to cut into Benjamin's bottom, and Sophie Ball and Niall Orange are pulling a face with how painful it must be for Benjamin!"

Sharon sighed with relief. "So, there's an even bigger trail of blood now, I don't know how Benjamin is going to sit down, he must be in agony, and his leg is still bleeding as well!"

Leon announced. "Joseph has appeared; he is trying to clean and dress Benjamin's bottom wound with a pan of warm water and some large leaves that he has found on a tree!"

Sharon gasped. "Joseph has lit a fire with a match; he is using the bottom of his pan to cauterise Benjamin's bottom to stop it from bleeding!"

Leon could not look. "By the way Benjamin is screaming, and Sophie Ball and Niall Orange are discussing that they think that Benjamin will not survive this because of a raised risk of infection!"

Sharon gipped. "That's making me feel squeamish, I can't imagine how Benjamin is feeling, he is screaming even louder, I don't know if he will survive the rest of the game from the amount of blood that he is losing!"

Leon pointed. "Look, Marie is walking towards Joseph, and Joseph has offered to cauterise Marie's arm as well!"

Sharon gasped. "Joseph is like a knight in shining armour fixing people;

Sophie Ball looks shocked because Joseph has helped Benjamin and Marie!"

Leon sounded shocked. "I wonder how Joseph thought of cauterising Benjamin and Marie's body parts, I think he is clever!"

Sharon sounded flabbergasted. "I am surprised that Joseph can help others because he has injured himself from being catapulted!"

Leon agreed. "Benjamin is bruised as well as he landed, and

Marie has got strawberry stains all over her from her diving into the strawberries and Marie has got a few splinters from making the sword!"

Sharon sounded surprised. "I am a bit shocked that Benjamin, Marie and Joseph are walking away in different directions unaided with nothing to help them walk, and at least Marie will smell sweet!"

Leon pointed. "Look, Emma is looking at all of the blood on the floor with a distraught look, she is looking very confused and obviously wondering what had happened!"

Sharon mentioned. "I think that Emma is in trouble because there is an army of beetles that are about to cover her from head to toe, and I don't mean a few, she needs to move now!"

Leon smirked. "I couldn't imagine anything worse; the beetles look horrible, I would hate them crawling on me, ooh heck, Sophie Ball is pulling a strange face with the tsunami of beetles covering Emma, I know that would be Emma's worst nightmare, and mine!"

Sharon screamed. "Ewe, Emma is getting totally covered by the black beetles because they are even entering inside of her ears, I think that she needs to get rid of them somehow before they take over her body, including her intimate parts!"

Leon gasped. "Look, Emma is using her pan to remove some of the beetles, Niall Orange has pointed a note out saying that the only way to get rid of the beetles is to stare at a person or an animal without blinking first!"

Sharon sounded puzzled. "So, Emma has got to stare someone out without blinking to win, what an odd challenge to stop yourself from getting covered in creepy crawly beetles!"

Leon sounded disappointed. "I would hate to have to stare someone out, I dread to think what will happen if Emma loses the game, look, Niall Orange and Sophie Ball are taking the piss out of the game because they're staring at each other and laughing!"

Sharon pointed. "Look, it looks like Ava has drawn the short straw because it looks like she is in some sort of trance with no expression on her face, and she is doing a kind of march as she walks over to Emma!"

Leon sounded serious. "Ava has come around back to her normal self again now, she is asking Emma how she appeared in front of her, Sophie Ball and Niall Orange are mocking Emma and Ava again by asking where they are, they are so daft!"

Sharon agreed. "Yes, they are daft, Ava is trying to run away from Emma who is covered in beetles, but it is like she has got superglue stuck to her feet because she is running on the spot, it looks quite funny actually and do you know what one firefly said to the other?"

Leon sounded deadly serious. "I don't know the answer, and Emma has explained the situation to Ava that they need to stare at each other, and they are now staring at each other!"

Sharon sounded upset. "The answer is you glow girl, and look, oh no, Ava has blinked, and all of the beetles are crawling away from Emma!"

Leon chuckled a little, shaking his head in disbelief. "Ava is walking down some steps disappearing into the floor, which means that Ava will be stuck in the darkroom and the orange button can get her out, it's a shame that Ava doesn't know that!"

Sharon sounded sad. "Niall Orange is announcing that day four of week two is over, and Sophie Ball is complaining that the game is flashing by too fast in front of her eyes!"

Leon listened to the violins. "They sound so nice and calming, and I feel disappointed that we didn't see the gold clock again!"

Sharon nodded. "Me too, and I am wondering if anyone will find the clock!"

Leon tried to sound positive. "We can go and enjoy sex in the spa or the swimming pool to make it a bit more exciting tomorrow if you like to cheer us up!"

Sharon smiled. "That is a big fat yes from me, we can do the sauna and the swimming pool!"

Leon and Sharon went to the local swimming pool with Leon speaking. "Ooh, this is exciting, the lifeguard has not noticed us yet playing with each other, the water must be a good camouflage, so we are okay to carry on fondling each other!"

Sharon turned red as a beetroot in the cheeks. "You spoke too soon, the lifeguard is whistling at us and telling us to leave the pool area immediately, let's try the sauna because it's empty!"

Chapter Twenty-One

English to Spanish

Leon started to finger Sharon's clit deeply with three fingers at the same time in a gentle swirling motion while stroking her hair with Leon speaking. "I am moving the bottom of your swimming costume to one side; I think that this is extremely exciting in a public area, filling your clit with my fingers!"

Sharon asked Leon. "Please fill me with your cock!"

An older lady in her late forties walked in, staring at Sharon and Leon speaking. "Is it my turn next, I could do with a bit of that to blow the cobwebs away down in my nether regions, you are both making it feel even steamier inside of this sauna!"

Leon laughed, speaking. "I think you can wish it was your turn my lovely, Sharon is my one, and only sweet, lucky lady who makes my wonderful world what it is, and full of mad passion and excitement, Sharon makes me steamy and hot, sorry but the answer is a no, I am going to ejaculate inside of you now Sharon!"

The random lady walked away moaning. "That's made me feel really erotic, I will have to find a man now who's willing to play with me!"

Sharon and Leon got up and walked away like nothing had happened, they noticed the older lady kissing a man outside of the changing room, they then did some food shopping and went home and made some food and chilled on the sofa until nine pm.

Sharon sounded happy. "The violins are playing again, that means that the game is about to start!"

Leon announced. "I can't believe it's day five of week two already!"

The cameras were focused on a poster for a few minutes, with Sharon reading it. "It says that if more trees are cut down, it could be irreversible the consequences meaning that it could not be sustained as a rainforest before we know it!"

Leon pulled a face, stretching his lips on either side of his face. "That's sad, but there isn't much we can do about it, I suppose!"

Sharon sounded concerned. "I hope that Ava is okay down in what I could call the dungeon because the darkroom is like that, and I bet it is dingy, cold, and damp!"

Leon sounded captivated. "Wow, look at Drew, it says on a note below his feet that he's got to learn some foreign words using an English-to-Spanish translation book that is next to the note and remember the words, but he can't open it until he's got an opponent to play against!"

Sharon noticed. "The book will not open until another person is at the side of Drew, and I am sure that Drew will find it a little hard to do that with him being South African!"

Leon agreed. "Yes, I think that you are correct Leon, look, Brandon is walking towards Drew!"

Sharon sounded positive. "At least Brandon is Scottish, so he has got more of a chance of learning new words because he has spoken English his whole life!"

Leon sounded upset. "Brandon is in a trance walking over to Drew, this is becoming a regular thing!"

Sharon sounded serious. "Look, Brandon has come around back to his normal self, and he's trying to get away, but he can't, he's running on the spot!"

Leon sounded frightened. "The book says that they have got five minutes to learn as many Spanish words as they can, then as the book closes, the person that says the most words in three minutes wins!"

Sharon had her eyes glued to the television. "The books have opened, Brandon and Drew look so nervous with them shaking with them both staring at the pages in detail with them only having one book between them!"

Leon announced his thoughts. "I guess they are both dreading losing, and Sophie Ball looks anxious!"

Sharon was focused. "The books have shut, and I have learnt a few new words in Spanish, I didn't know that huevo is egg in Spanish!"

Leon sounded interested. "I didn't know that jelly is gelatina in Spanish either!"

Sharon listened. "Niall Orange and Sophie Ball are announcing that Brandon is the winner!"

Leon sounded concerned. "Drew has disappeared, I bet Drew is in the darkroom with Ava, at least there are two of them in there now!"

Sharon suggested. "I just hope that Ava works out that she needs to press the orange button to release herself and maybe Drew as well if he is touching her as she presses the button!"

Leon shrugged his shoulders. "We can hope that Ava realises what the orange button does!"

Sharon sounded upset. "Look, Brandon has thrown the Spanish book on the floor in a rage! "

Leon rolled his eyes. "I would probably have done the same, and Brandon is yelling no as he is walking away!"

Sharon sounded shocked. "Look, Amelia and Joseph have appeared; they are looking at the Spanish book that Brandon has left behind!"

Leon took in an intake of air; he then let it out fast. "Oh no, a note has appeared next to the Spanish book, it says on it that the person that puts the most posters up within a minute will win, this is getting a bit repetitive, these games are so cringey!"

Sharon signed by pointing. "Some posters have appeared between Amelia and Joseph with foam written on them!"

Leon laughed. "This game is silly, they have only got a few bars of chewing gum to chew, they have got to use that to stick the posters onto the trees and that's included in the minute!"

Sharon sounded surprised. "A minute isn't really long enough, wow, look, there's foam leaving the middle of the posters that Amelia and Joseph have put up, the foam is starting to make the floor slippery as they are chewing the gum and attempting to put the posters up!"

Leon laughed. "It's funny the way Amelia and Joseph are falling all over, it is like one step forward and three steps back!"

Sharon gasped. "It looks like Amelia has lost because she has disappeared, I am not surprised because she only managed to put two posters up, and Joseph only managed to put three up!"

Leon sounded sad. "So, Ava, Drew and Amelia are all stuck in the darkroom now!"

Sharon sounded disappointed. "Oh shucks, Niall Orange and Sophie

Ball have announced that day five of week two has finished!"

Leon suggested. "Let's go and play darts at our local pub tomorrow!"

Sharon smiled. "That sounds like a nice and fun idea!"

Leon picked Sharon up and carried her upstairs. "Now that I have gently put you on the bed, I will gently caress your body from head to toe!"

Chapter Twenty-Two

Pub Challenge

Sharon sounded intrigued. "So, I love the way that you talk with your hands and dance, you don't need to do anything to turn me on, but you always amazingly make me erotically turned on, what else are you going to do?"

Leon winked. "I love how confident you are and how you make

me feel like I am the most amazing person in the world!"

Sharon wiped a tear from her eye. "I love the way that you kiss me and flirt and touch me, you make my body tingle with excitement!"

Leon groaned. "I love looking into your eyes and the way that you tickle me softly with your nails!"

Sharon giggled. "This is a lovely conversation; you make me have butterflies in my stomach when we touch and talk together!"

Leon sniffed up. "I love the way that you smell, and I love us sharing ice cream together!"

Sharon walked downstairs for some ice cream. "I knew that we would enjoy this ice cream together, you are so generous when you tip people for making us nice food!"

Leon smiled. "Now that we have enjoyed our ice cream, let's make love together, I can't resist you anymore, you are my smooth operator and creamy gemstone!"

Sharon grabbed Leon. "I am loving pulling your warm horny fit body towards me, the way you have gently slipped your dick inside of me warms my heart, I am enjoying every thrust inside of me!"

Leon screeched. "I can feel my heart beating faster with it beating out of my chest and my penis is that hard you could use it as a towel rail!"

Sharon sounded erotic. "My nipples are so hard, please suck them hard before you ejaculate because I can feel your creamy load coming!"

Leon agreed. "I can't hold back any longer, I am filling you with my love juices!"

Sharon sighed. "I can feel it penetrating inside of me, it feels like a well-needed key in the door!"

Leon stroked Sharon as they started to calm down with Leon speaking. "We can slowly drop off to sleep, then enjoy our darts tomorrow!"

Sharon and Leon slept well, they then enjoyed their darts session in the local pub, and they relaxed together with a romantic spaghetti bolognese with Sharon announcing. "Yay, it's the moment that we have been waiting for, day six of week two is starting, and the violins sound relaxing!"

Leon gasped. "I can't believe it's that time again already!"

Sharon held Leon's hand. "I can't think of anybody better to spend my time with Leon, look, Marie is trying to enter inside of a pub bar door unsuccessfully that has appeared from the air, what a strange thing to appear in a jungle!"

Leon sounded puzzled. "Maybe the gold clock is in there, and there will be some kind of catch because they don't do anything nice in this game!"

Sharon agreed. "Marie has pushed her way inside; it looks like a normal pub; it looks a bit eerie; something is bound to happen for the worst!"

Leon shook with fright. "There are hissing snakes surrounding Marie, I don't know how she is going to get away without being bitten!"

Sharon was concentrating on Marie. "Look, Marie has got her scissors in one hand and her pen in the other hand, she is trying to kill them, and she sadly never managed to get to the bar for a drink!"

Leon sounded frustrated. "Marie's Brummie accent makes her sound even more stressed, I think!"

Sharon sounded shocked. "It says on a drinking glass at the bar, 'Drink me when all of the snakes have been cooked, with or without help!"

Leon gasped. "I don't know how Marie is going to burn all of the snakes alone!"

Sharon sounded down. "Marie is about to be bitten by a snake, and Emma has just walked into the pub, and she has used her mirrors reflection from the sun to start a fire again to help to kill all of the snakes!"

Leon sounded sad. "Marie has been bitten; she will probably die!"

Sharon wiped a tear from her eye. "Emma has helped Marie out of the snake-filled pub, that is kind of Emma to do that!"

Leon turned the television volume up. "I think the snake missed biting Marie by the way she is talking, if she was bitten, she wouldn't be talking, she would be screaming by now or lifeless and then dead!"

Sharon looked Marie up and down. "I think Marie is lucky to be out of there alive!"

Leon agreed. "I know, Marie could have died in there, I think that Emma is Marie's saviour!"

Sharon looked at a glass leaving the pub. "Wow, Marie's drink is hovering in the air on a tray travelling towards Marie and Emma, I think that's amazing, and Niall Orange can't get his head around it either!"

Leon sounded full of love. "That's lovely of Marie to share her drink with Emma, it sounds like it was a drink of lemonade with specks of burnt bits in it, or that's what Niall Orange is saying!"

Sharon sounded full of happiness. "Marie is sharing a cooked snake with Emma, at least they have got plenty to eat and a positive end to a bad experience!"

Emma thanked Marie. "Thank you for sharing your snake with me!"

Marie nodded up and down. "You're welcome!"

Leon agreed. "That's nice of them to share, and Sophie Ball sounds a little teary!"

Sharon pointed with her eyes lit up. "Wow, look, Ava is walking behind Emma and Marie!"

Leon sounded shocked. "Sophie Ball is suggesting that Ava must have pressed the orange button!"

Sharon guessed. "It must have released just Ava from the darkroom!"

Leon looked at Ava. "It looks like the light is hurting Ava's eyes with her shielding her eyes from the sunlight, and I don't blame Emma and Marie for walking away, they look a little more content now that they have enjoyed their lemonade!"

Chapter Twenty-Three

Red Chainsaw Drone

Sharon sounded a little puzzled. "So, that's Amelia and Drew that are still stuck in the darkroom now, is that correct, and I am not surprised that Ava's eyes are finding it hard to adjust to the light again because immediately moving from dark to light must be distressing?"

Leon sounded unfolded. "I wouldn't want to be any of them, I hate it when people use big words instead of simple ones because they sound hard, my big word is capricious, it means that you like something one minute and you don't like it the next!"

Sharon looked up and down. "It's like the volunteer contestants playing the game that we are watching, I bet they don't mind it when the good parts happen, and they hate it when it goes wrong!"

Leon crossed his arms. "Yes, that is true!"

Sharon laughed. "Yes, I bet they feel dirty like they need a good wash, I know that is how I would feel!"

Leon sounded unsettled. "Look, Benjamin is in some sort of trance, and there is a paintbrush in front of him with some paint at the side of the brush!"

Sharon pointed. "Benjamin is at the point of no return; there's a note saying that he has got to paint a square on the floor in front of him before a moving line gets to the middle of the square!"

Leon sounded puzzled. "Oh heck, a brown wooden square has appeared, Niall Orange is commenting that the square is roughly about sixty centimetres each way, so, my understanding is that if the line on the floor moves on its own to the middle of the square before he has painted the square something will happen to him!"

Sharon sounded worried. "It says that the whole square has got to be completely painted in black with no gaps, I wonder what will happen to Benjamin if he doesn't paint it in time?"

Benjamin sounded nervous, playing with his hands. "This game gets scarier!"

Leon sounded engrossed. "We will find out in a few minutes if he finishes painting the square or not!"

Sharon sounded upset. "I love Benjamin's American accent, his leg and bottom still look painful from the chainsaw cutting him, and it wasn't good when he was chased by a red chainsaw drone either!"

Leon sounded in suspense. "Benjamin looks like he is back to normal, but he has started painting the square!"

Sharon sounded distraught. "Look, the red line is moving slowly from the opposite side of where Benjamin is painting, the line is moving on its own working towards the middle of the square, and I can't help thinking about how I felt scared for him when he was chasing away the chainsaw drone, and especially when the falling knife just missed hitting him!"

Leon sounded disturbed. "In my opinion, Benjamin has got no chance of painting the square in time because the line seems to be moving towards him faster, and he's not putting the black paint on fast enough to win the red line, and he has luckily escaped death a few times now, and that arrow that nearly hit him would have freaked me out!"

Niall Orange and Sophie Ball can not make up their minds what the results will be with Sharon gulping. "When he was robbed of his match, that was like pulling a sticking plaster off compared to him struggling with his pain from his leg and his bottom!"

Leon agreed. "Yes, I really do think that Joseph was kind cauterising Benjamin's bottom and Marie's arm, and it looks like Benjamin is fucked because the red line is nearly in the middle of the square, and he has still got the top of the square to paint!"

Sharon pulled a face, pulling her jaw downward. "Oh dear, a piece of paper has appeared with Amelia and Drew written on it, and it says to point at a name so Benjamin has definitely lost by the look of it, Sophie Ball also sounds intrigued about what will happen next!"

Leon gasped. "In my opinion, I think that Benjamin has got to choose Amelia or Drew to swap within the darkroom because the red line has stopped in the middle of the square, and the paintbrush has released that much boiling heat into the handle making it impossible for Benjamin to hold it anymore, so he has dropped the paintbrush because it was burning his hand and I think that we need to brush up on the laughs!"

Sharon smiled, putting her hand up to her mouth in suspense. "Benjamin has chosen to swap places with Amelia, it's a shame that he has dropped the orange button back onto the floor because he didn't know that it would release people in the darkroom, he has been in the darkroom once for getting pulled into the water, it looks like he is back in the darkroom again!"

Leon sounded shocked. "Amelia has appeared from the air, and she has landed on the hot ground, and Benjamin has disappeared down some steps, so I guess that Benjamin is in the darkroom with Drew!"

Sharon agreed. "Yes, I wonder if Benjamin will be catapulted into the air out of the darkroom again!"

Leon swallowed a large intake of air. "Amelia looks like she is getting used to the light again with her shielding her eyes with her blinking heavily, and I guess that Benjamin's bag full of nothing may help him and Drew if they have a panic attack!"

Sharon gasped for air. "Look, Brandon is looking up into the clouds because bubbles are floating up into the sky!"

Leon shook his head. "This place gets worse; a note has appeared from a bubble that has popped above Joseph's head saying that Brandon and Joseph have got to catch the bubbles, and it says that the person that catches the most bubbles in ten minutes wins!"

Sharon watched Brandon and Joseph. "I can't believe that they have got to catch bubbles, this is a childish but fun activity, I think that it will be hard because the bubbles will travel upwards so fast if it's windy and burst with joy!"

Leon absorbed everything in. "Joseph is catching the most bubbles; I think the bubbles look so light and fluffy cool, and do you know why bubbles can not ever tell secrets?"

Sharon sounded puzzled. "I don't know, and Brandon isn't doing bad either at catching the bubbles, I really do think this is going to be a draw!"

Leon cried. "The answer is, because they always pop under pressure and look, an extra-large adult bubble with a door to enter inside of has appeared!"

Sharon's face dropped. "That means that either Brandon or Joseph will probably have to enter into the bubble, I would hate to walk inside of that bubble because it would get too hot for a start with the sun beaming down!"

Leon sounded upset. "At least there is a breathing hole in the top of the see-through bubble so that whoever goes inside will have some air, even if it is unbearable boiling air!"

Sharon sounded distraught. "Brandon's name is written on a note that has just fallen next to his feet from another bubble that has popped, it says that Brandon needs to go inside of the bubble!"

Leon sounded astounded. "I can't believe that Brandon has just walked into the bubble, and the door has shut behind him locking him inside, he must feel so hot and sweaty already!"

Sharon sounded amazed. "Joseph is walking off from the bubble crying, and the gold clock is in the grass near to his feet, but his tears must be distorting his vision, so he didn't notice it!"

Chapter Twenty-Four

Tied Up

Leon sounded disappointed. "Never mind, at least the clock is still there, and Sophie Ball is announcing that it's the end of day six of week two with the closing screen showing a large whiteboard message hanging from a tree while the violins are playing a creepy tune!"

Sharon sounded heartbroken. "There's a photo of a forest fire, it says that they're being destroyed this way as well, and the cameras have just shown Brandon in the bubble, he is wet through with sweat, how horrible!"

Leon sounded low-spirited. "Yeah, nature can be cruel and disrespectfully devastating, it will be the heat that's caused the fires, and I don't think that Brandon will survive in there much longer!"

Sharon kissed Leon on his forehead. "I love you so much, please kiss me all over on the sofa, I love it when you kiss me!"

Leon kissed Sharon. "I love kissing you from head to toe!"

Sharon groaned. "I am not sure which part of my body I am enjoying you kissing the most!"

Leon suggested. "Let's go to Scarborough and hire a surfboard and enjoy surfboarding tomorrow in the sea, it will be fun riding the waves!"

Sharon laughed. "Whatever, I will try not to fall off!"

Leon smiled. "I think that it will be a laugh, this is turning me on so much kissing you, I think that we need some ice to cool us down!"

Sharon chuckled. "No, we need to get hotter under the collar!"

Leon lay on the floor at the front of the fire. "I think we should lie here for a while and play with each other; I have brought my handcuffs for us to play with, I will cuff you to the bottom of the coffee table if you like while I play with you!"

Sharon willingly got tied up. "This makes it more fun, as you are licking my clit, it's making me want your dick inside of me!"

Leon slid his penis inside of Sharon's clit. "I love thrusting inside of you, your black hole is the best thing ever!"

Sharon giggles. "We could enjoy sex on our surfboard tomorrow; I think that would be fun!"

Leon agreed. "Oh yeah, that would be awesome, I can't hold my sperm back any longer!"

Sharon shut her eyes, enjoying every bit of Leon's spunky juices spurting inside of her clit. "Now that we have shared our love, let's go to bed!"

Leon removed the handcuffs, and they went to bed and enjoyed sexy play on the surfboard the next day with Leon speaking. "We have got the attention of the whole of Scarborough beach, and the television cameras!"

Sharon smiled. "At least we have had a memorable day to remember forever because it will be on every social media platform that you can think of!"

Leon drove back to Sharon's house, and they enjoyed some food and a hot shower together with Leon speaking. "Well, it's the best time of day again!"

Sharon turned the television on. "Day seven of week two is starting with the violins playing a rich, sweet and vibrant tone!"

Leon looked at the opening screen of a whiteboard. "It says that the trees are being cut down for paper, wood, mainly soy and palm oil and eating locally sourced foods helps because it doesn't use fuel to transport it as far, and we can all help to make our future better for the people left behind!"

Sharon scratched her toe. "Looking after the environment is good!"

Leon sounds excited. "Amelia is being pulled in front of a dartboard, it says on a note above the dartboard that she can release Benjamin and Drew from the darkroom and Brandon from inside of the bubble if any of her ten darts hit their names, and if it hits any other name, the persons name that it hits, that person swaps places with Benjamin and Drew!"

Sharon sat staring. "Wow, Amelia is throwing her first dart, and it's fallen onto the ground, what a waste of the first dart!"

Leon sounded distraught." I am desperate to know what will happen next!"

Sharon nodded. "Me too, Amelia is throwing her second dart, she is a rubbish thrower because it's just hit a flying pretty pink butterfly in mid-air!"

Leon sounded nervous. "Poor butterfly, I wonder if this third dart will hit the dartboard?"

Sharon laughed. "Wow, Amelia's third dart has hit Drew's name, I wonder how he will be let out of the darkroom!"

Leon looked behind the dartboard, startled. "I am surprised Amelia hit Drew's name, never mind the board because she will never be a top dart player, Look, Drew is flying through the air, I suppose that's just standard for this place!"

Sharon laughed. "That's another injury to add to Drew's long list of ailments!"

Leon could not believe what he was hearing. "Sophie Ball is calling Drew the flying Drew; this game gets dafter!"

Sharon laughed. "That's the first nickname of many to come, I bet!"

Leon bit his nail. "It's making me feel nervous, I am dreading where Amelia's fourth dart will end up!"

Sharon laughed. "Amelia's fourth dart has hit a white-tailed deer, I don't know how she managed that, at least it is something to cook if they catch it because the dart will slow it down, the poor thing!"

Leon agreed. "I can't tell if Amelia is getting better or worse at throwing the darts!"

Sharon blinked heavily. "I am not sure if I can watch the fifth dart, this feels so stressful!"

Leon put his hand up at his face with a small gap between his fingers. "Me too, this is so painful, Amelia is so clumsy with the darts, or she is too nervous with her hands shaking so much!"

Sharon gasped. "Amelia's fifth dart has hit a large chimpanzee behind the dartboard, and it's baby chimpanzee is running towards its mother; this is so tear-jerking, it is hard to watch!"

Leon wiped a tear from Sharon's cheek. "Seriously, Amelia couldn't hit something if it landed in front of her nose, I guess!"

Chapter Twenty-Five

Bubble

Sharon chuckled. "I think I am going to nickname her dopey Amelia!"

Leon breathed heavily. "I feel sorry for the baby chimpanzee, I don't know what will happen now, I am sure the baby chimpanzee will mingle in with the other animals!"

Sharon gasped. "Amelia is throwing her sixth dart; I hope she throws better this time, and I heard that a dart went to the doctors because it wasn't feeling sharp enough!"

Leon shook his head. "Amelia's sixth dart has hit the edge of the dartboard, and it's now fallen onto the floor, and I bet if a dartboard could speak, it would say to a dart that it didn't look sharp enough!"

Sharon smirked. "I can't believe that Amelia is throwing her seventh dart already, I would feel so scared to be anywhere near to Amelia right now!"

Leon's eyes lit up. "I just want to know if anyone else is released, or being put into the darkroom, Amelia's hands look so sweaty!"

Sharon grunted. "We are about to find out, oh no, Joseph was walking past the dartboard as Amelia threw her seventh dart!"

Leon gasped. "I know, it was supposed to be a name on the dartboard, not a person in real life,

Joseph has fallen to the floor with his finger getting the brunt of the stabbing dart piercing his skin, he looks and sounds like he is in crippling pain, Sophie Ball is pulling a face!"

Sharon wiped a tear from her eye. "Amelia is crying, I am not surprised that she is crying because of what she has just done to Joseph, Niall Orange looks like he is going to be sick with the look of Joseph's finger looking so bloody!"

Leon pulled a face. "If I were Joseph, I would do a one hundred and eighty and disappear fast before he is injured any more!"

Sharon laughed. "I like that, I don't think Amelia could ever score one hundred and eighty!"

Leon rolled his eyes. "Amelia may hit the dartboard with dart eight, hopefully!"

Sharon laughed. "I doubt it, at least she has managed to release Drew from the darkroom!"

Leon sounded tense. "Wow, Amelia has actually managed to hit Benjamin's name with dart eight, that means that Benjamin will most probably be flying through the air any time now from the darkroom!"

Sharon's eyes lit up. "Wow, that means that the darkroom is empty up to now, there is just Brandon to get out of the bubble now, he may be safer in the bubble, but I am sure that he will be hungry, feeling trapped, thrust-rated and frightened!"

Leon agreed. "Yes, I would feel devastated if I was Brandon!"

Sharon kept interest. "Oh no, Amelia is throwing her ninth dart, and she has hit Ava's name on the dartboard, I bet Ava has ended up in the darkroom or she has taken Brandon's place in the large bubble!"

Leon looked at the sky. "Did you see Benjamin fly through the air screaming just then? That's more bruising and damage for him to deal with, he must hate landing!"

Sharon sounded concerned. "They must be all fed up and want out, I know I would!"

Leon nodded. "Me too, let's watch Amelia throw her final dart number ten, I wonder what will happen with this dart because she is unpredictable, the way she is going, half of the jungle will be dead the way she's throwing them!"

Sharon concentrated. "Yes, true and blunt darts are pointless, look, blooming heck, Amelia has actually hit a puma that reminds me of a cat a little, it was creeping up towards her with her last number ten dart!"

Leon sounded relieved. "At least it will not eat her now because the puma is injured, I am sort of glad that this pain game is only on for six weeks because they are taking over a jungle full of dangerous animals, it's not fair on the animals I suppose either with humans invading their personal space!"

Sharon's ears pricked up. "It looks like Amelia can go because she has run out of darts, and she is walking away, and Sophie Ball is commenting on how dramatic Amelia's dart game was!"

Leon sounded upset. "The television cameras are focusing on Ava being stuck inside of the bubble!"

Sharon laughed. "Did you know that a bubble wanted to go to the theatre to watch a pop concert?"

Leon chuckled. "Oh, bubble off, we are daft!"

Sharon sounded disappointed. "Niall Orange has just announced that it's the end of week two and the beginning of week three tomorrow and he is dancing along to the violins!"

Leon smiled. "You remind me of my glass of wine because you are classy and smooth, and I love to savour every moment with you!"

Sharon smiled. "You are my Prince Charming and my gentle smooth operator, everything that you do is perfect in every way!"

Leon stroked Sharon's hair. "You are so beautiful, I love you so much, your hair feels so sexy and soft!"

Sharon kissed Leon passionately. "You are such a wonderful kisser, please kiss my clit after kissing all of the way down to it!"

Leon kissed downwards. "If this sofa could talk, it would say how much fun we are having!"

Sharon expressed her opinion. "I would love to enter into the game just for the money!"

Leon laughed. "I would love to enter for the money as well, but I think it's a bad idea with what has happened to them so far!"

Sharon sounded serious. "Yeah, I actually like living too much to enter into the game!"

Leon sounded clear. "In reality, we have got another proper couple of weeks off work, then we have got to go back, so we couldn't enter into the game even if we wanted to because we wouldn't get paid if it runs over six weeks so that we can live comfortably!"

Sharon murmured. "Yes, I get what you are meaning that we don't have much choice in the matter, but if we won the jackpot, we wouldn't have to work again if we could talk our workplaces into giving us extra annual leave!"

Chapter Twenty-Six

Poster Hung

Leon undressed Sharon. "Or we could beg for extra time off work even if it's unpaid, and I am sorry, but there's no point in talking about this because we can't enter into the game, anyway!"

Sharon sounded disappointed. "I suppose not, get your kit off because you need to fill my pleasures today!"

Leon stripped off, then stripped Sharon. "Ooh, I love it when you are assertive, it turns me on!"

Sharon laughed. "Please go down there and suck my breasts, I really do need your warm lubricated mouth around them!"

Leon sucked Sharon's breasts for a while. "Can I fill you with my dick now, please?"

Sharon laughed. "Of course, you can get it stuck inside of me!"

Leon pushed hard inside of Sharon's clit. "I love how warm and wet you are, I am going to have to ejaculate because I can't hold it back anymore!"

Sharon pulled Leon's bottom closer. "That's amazing, and that's one of the coolest things ever!"

Leon suggested. "Let's go to the horse racing event in York tomorrow!"

Sharon agreed, they slept and enjoyed a full day betting on many horses winning spare change, they then sat down and put the television on at nine pm with Sharon sounding giggly. "Sophie Ball is excited with day one of week three starting and Niall Orange sounds full of joy as well with the violins playing!"

Leon put his beer on Sharon's lounge coffee table. "Wow, Niall Orange is inviting people from home to join in!"

Sharon nodded up and down. "Yes, in person, and Sophie has announced that they will pick anybody who watches the pain game from home that applies to enter the game by email!"

Leon sounded jumpy. "I suppose the main reason is to make it more interesting, anyone that is picked at random can enter into the jungle, if anybody gets removed for any reason from the jungle in the near future, I suppose the new volunteer will take their place!"

Sharon sounded over giddy, fidgeting with her hands. "Do you think we should apply for the pain game show, what do you think?"

Leon sniggered, sounding a little down. "We would have to ask our work first, but if they say yes that would be great so that we can have longer than six weeks if we need it, we can enter because Sophie Ball has mentioned that it is a form that you fill in on the pain game website for a chance to enter into the pain game!"

Sharon suggested. "I beg you, let's just apply, then if we do get picked and get the chance to enter into the jungle, we can worry about our workplaces later!"

Leon nodded. "You have finally twisted my arm, okay, we will apply!"

Sharon laughed. "It didn't take much twisting, thank you, we will apply tomorrow, let's just see what happens tonight!"

Leon laughed. "It says on a poster hung on a tree on the opening screen that a Jaguar only eats meat, I think this is obvious, everyone should know that!"

Sharon chuckled. "We even knew that answer!"

Leon gasped. "Emma is wandering around; it says on a large note attached to a tree that she needs to learn how to remove wool from a sheep!"

Sharon sounded devastated. "I wouldn't know where to start, and I know that I am changing the subject, but I bet Ava has released herself with her orange button!"

Leon's eyes slowly turned towards Sharon. "Yeah, I am sure that Ava is out of the bubble by now!"

Sharon kissed Leon. "Emma has got to strip all of the wool from the sheep without making it bleed or run away!"

Leon sounded puzzled. "This is a strange thing to do, I am sure there will be more instructions soon, and I dread to know what will happen if Emma can't skin the sheep!"

Sharon spoke her mind. "Like Sophie Ball is saying, it is only a matter of time before one of them will be out dead or alive!"

Leon nodded. "Sophie Ball is correct; this may even be Emma's last day, Emma has at least helped Marie out of the pub, been covered in beetles, and had her bottom stuck in a slide!"

Sharon sounded positive. "Yeah, at least she has stayed alive to do all that, Emma has also had sex with Ava in Ava's pop-up tent, and she noticed

Brandon's torch light facing upwards, and she has also made something with a chainsaw to release Brandon from the strawberries, and she has been in the private safe room, I think that she is lucky to be alive and experience things that other people will never do!"

Leon stared at the screen. "Emma is just sitting on the floor waiting next to the sheep, it is like she is waiting for something to happen, I am just thinking she has also slipped on high tree branches to play the piano in mid-air with no safety gear to keep her safe!"

Sharon sounded shocked. "Emma has been delivered a knife by a drone with a flat surface on top of its body with a note under the knife saying that she has got to skin the sheep herself, while we are waiting for her to think about skinning the sheep, I am just thinking about how Emma had hit Brandon on the head with a pan, she can be brutal, and she also used her mirror to start a fire, she is a tough cookie!"

Leon reassured Emma. "Emma is a Yorkshire lass, she will easily do it, I am more confident that she can skin a sheep like eating a bag of chips!"

Sharon nodded. "Yeah, Emma has already started to skin the sheep, I want to know what she gets if she succeeds in her goal!"

Leon smirked. "It looks like Emma is getting angry with the sheep because it's trying to run away from her!"

Sharon chuckled. "This looks a little bit funny with her fighting with the sheep, I think that she needs an extra pair of hands because she looks to be losing her grip, but nobody is appearing to help her, and I am just thinking, what do you call a flock of sheep falling down a hillside?"

Leon looked blank. "I wish that I knew!"

Sharon answered. "A lamb slide!"

Leon smiled, pulling a face. "I am really not surprised; they probably don't want to die!"

Sharon sounded surprised. "Joseph is walking over to help Emma; that's kind of him!"

Leon grumbled. "I would love for us to be there, but sadly, that will never happen!"

Chapter Twenty-Seven

Parrots

Sharon sounded grateful. "I think that Joseph is a good person helping Emma!"

Leon smiled. "Emma is more than halfway done shearing the sheep compared to how she was managing alone!"

Sharon agreed. "I just hope that Emma gets something nice if she wins by completing her goal!"

Leon screeched. "Wow, Emma has finished shearing the sheep, and a pile of raspberries has just fallen from a drone that had the knife on it, this is an odd thing to happen, but it's better than a bad thing happening for a change!"

Sharon glowed with happiness. "This is a nice reward, Emma is sharing her raspberries with Joseph, Joseph has worked hard as well, I think he deserves to share the raspberries with Emma because that was a dangerous, hair-raising situation!"

Leon's eyes lit up. "Well, you know what we will be buying tomorrow, don't you?"

Sharon guessed. "Raspberries, I guess, am I correct?"

Leon's eyes lit up. "Yes, I think that would be nice, the thought of this is making my mouth water!"

Sharon blinked a lot. "Wow, Ava is walking past Emma and Joseph with the orange button in her hand, we said that she would probably use it to release her!"

Leon sounded joyful. "I am glad that Ava has got out of the bubble!"

Sharon's eyes twinkled. "I am happy for Ava as well!"

Leon sounded devastated. "Oh shucks, Sophie Ball has just announced the end of day one of week three, and the violins are playing softly!"

Sharon sounded distressed. "It's gone so fast this episode, at least we will enjoy our raspberries tomorrow!"

Leon suggested. "We could go to the Crumbs sandwich shop because they do a raspberry smoothie and a raspberry cheesecake that we can enjoy for our dessert!"

Sharon nodded. "Yes, I need something as sweet as you, then we can tell our work that we need extra time off!"

Leon laughed. "I am a police constable, so there are plenty of people to cover me, so I should be okay for another few weeks off until the pain game has ended!"

Sharon pulled a face. "I just hope my bartender job lets me have more time off as well!"

Leon and Sharon enjoyed their food, they then got approved for more time from work, and they then enjoyed a walk around Sandal castle, they then enjoyed a coffee at the end of their walk in the castle café, they then watched a film.

Leon sounded relaxed. "We have had a lovely, relaxing and fun day, let's get busy on the sofa while we are waiting for the pain game to start!"

Sharon started to strip Leon. "At least we have got the time off that we need from work, I am loving sucking your cock!"

Leon slowly stripped Sharon as well. "I love your body; it turns me on so much, you are making me feel like ejaculating into your mouth!"

Sharon's eyes looked up towards Leon's with her struggling to talk. "Do it, and I will swallow it, every part of you is amazing!"

Leon ejaculated into Sharon's mouth. "Thank you for letting me do that Sharon, you are my proper ray of sunshine, and my rainbow of joy!"

Sharon smiled. "You're welcome, I will just brush my teeth, and then the pain game will be starting, I am so excited to find out what today's activities hold!"

Leon sat down on the sofa in his jogging bottoms. "Sharon, you need to sit down because day two of week three is about to start because the violins are playing, and I think they sound a little bit screechy like they are screaming at us today!"

Sharon sounded intrigued. "I can't wait to see what's happening, this game is so dramatic and draining of my energy!"

Leon looked up at a fact hanging from a tree. "It says that the scarlet macaw parrots are one of many large birds and it is famous and fondly known as rainbows of the forest with a striking plumage, which has got predominantly red, yellow, and light blue feathers with plenty of vocal mimicry!

Sharon pulled a sour face. "I am not over-keen on birds!"

Leon pointed. "Birds are not my favourite animal either, but they sound like beautifully naturally made pretty birds, and I know it's so emotionally changing this place, look, Marie is getting dragged towards some material and a sewing machine!"

Sharon beamed with a strange look. "I just hope that Marie can sow and if she can't, she will have to learn how to sew fast!"

Leon sounded cheery. "I am glad that it's not me having to sew something because it would look like a dog's dinner if I attempted to make anything, and it would have me in stitches bobbing along!"

Sharon sounded in a good mood. "I bet that's cock and wool; you would work it out!"

Leon laughed. "I would rather buy some suits because I know where I can buy four suits for a pound!"

Sharon shook her head in disbelief. "Don't be daft!"

Leon sounded jolly. "I just need to buy a deck of cards, and it looks like Marie has got to make a doll pattern and stuff it; I didn't know that the filling of dolls would be a blood red colour, I bet that will stress Marie out!"

Sharon sounded made up. "I wasn't thinking of that kind of suit, and I think the end result of the doll will be cute when it is finished!"

Leon sounded edgy and cautious. "Yeah, so long as it doesn't come and try to attack people, it makes me wonder if this is why they are recruiting for new people to enter into the game!"

Sharon sounded anxious. "Yeah, I agree, they probably would make the doll come alive in this game, it's so unpredictable, you can never tell what's going to happen next, it is really crazy and creepy in an addictive way making us want more!"

Chapter Twenty-Eight

Bungee Cord

Leon glared at Marie. "I think Marie is doing a great job of making the doll!"

Sharon sounded miserable. "Marie is only making the doll because she has been made to, and I think its eyes look full of evil already with them turning black even though they were made blue!"

Leon's ears pricked up. "Niall Orange is encouraging people to send extra money into the game towards the prize fund so that the players will get more savvy at killing each other, I wonder what the prize fund is now?"

Sharon quizzed Leon. "What do you think? I think we should send some money in, we will get it back maybe if we end up in the game so that we can encourage other people watching the game to put more money into it as well to make the price fund larger, so that more people will watch the pain game because more people will be talking about it!"

Leon shook with shock. "Yeah, I suppose so, look, it's a staggering twenty-five trillion pounds in the prize pot now, there will definitely not be eight people left by the end of the pain game, I am one hundred percent sure on that because they will most probably murder each other for the money!"

Sharon stated. "Niall Orange has just told the players by using a megaphone about the twenty-five trillion pounds that are locked in the bank safely waiting for the last players standing to share at the end of week six!"

Leon cried with happiness. "I have never seen a group of people as cheerful in my life on the television in such a miserable situation, and I hope that we get picked to enter into the pain game!"

Sharon sounded desperate. "I am not surprised they are happy; I definitely would be knowing that I could win that amount of money, I really do want to go into the pain game and hide from everybody so that I stay alive to get the money!"

Leon yelled. "Yeah, but think about it, when you have got that pain-enhancing needle bringing pain back that you have had through your whole life up to now, that sounds bad, especially the pain when you had your breast removed due to breast cancer and look, the doll that Marie is making, it's hands are starting to move, and it's got a massive creepy grin on its face!"

Sharon bellowed. "Oh my gosh, I suppose you are right, look, the doll is moving its lips now, it's definitely alive, and kicking with a strong heartbeat with it breathing better than most of them in the jungle at the moment!"

Leon sounded flabbergasted. "The doll has just spoken; it's announced that it's going to kill people, this is very frightening with a chill running down my spine to hear this news!"

Sharon had the sound of dread in her voice. "Oh no, I wonder how a doll can kill someone, and the doll has started to creepily sing, it's my cue to kill everyone around me, it is singing!"

Leon sounded distraught. "We will probably find out any minute, look Marie's hand is shaking badly, and she is refusing to put the last stitch in the doll with what it has just said!"

Sharon sounded hysterical. "The doll has started to stand up, it has just breathed on Marie, and she is lying lifeless on the floor, it must be something that the doll has been made out of that has made Marie collapse!"

Leon's eyes lit up. "You are probably correct; I think that the doll is going to kill them all!"

Sharon wiped a tear from her eye. "That's Marie out of the game; the doll is definitely on a mission to kill!"

Leon sounded frightened. "Yeah, I think that you are correct, they need to run while they are able to!"

Sharon sounded astounded. "It's like the doll is teasing and challenging Emma by running after her but not killing her yet, and her panicked Yorkshire accent is so strong, and that creepy singing is scary!"

Leon sounded thunderstruck. "The doll is sending one of its eyes towards Emma, it's like it's on a bungee cord getting ready to catch and real her in!"

Sharon gasped. "It's like the doll wants to control Emma with it not killing her yet, the dolls eyes are looking into Emma's eyes while she's running!"

Leon sounded confused. "I have never seen a dolls eye still attached to the dolls body by a bungee cord chasing someone before!"

Sharon sounded spaced out. "Me neither, this game is strange!"

Leon pointed. "Drew is watching the dolls every move; he is definitely onto it!"

Sharon stared at Emma. "Look, flying Drew has threaded a needle on his sewing kit, he is sewing and attaching it to a tree by tying it onto the tree!"

Leon gasped. "Look, Drew is definitely up to something because he has just walked past the doll, and he has stabbed into it's back with the needle; the needle has inserted a stitch attaching the doll to the tree, which will hopefully stop it in its tracks!"

Sharon sounded intense. "The dolls eye has re-attached to its eye socket, and it is trying to break the cotton to get away, that cotton must be really strong because it's not broken as yet!"

Leon sounded relieved. "I am glad that Drew and Emma are walking away from the tied-up doll before it gets loose!"

Sharon concentrated with her eyes fixed on the doll. "The doll is stronger than it looks, I think that it's going to break free any moment, the doll has killed Marie, we don't want any more being killed by the red stuffing from the doll!"

Leon had a shiver down his spine. "The thought of Marie's parents left behind without a daughter sounds extremely distressing to me, and I will miss that unique Brummie accent!"

Sharon bit her nails with her nerves. "Yeah, I will miss Marie's Birmingham Brummie accent as well, I think a few more people will be killed in a minute because the cotton is shredding!"

Leon sounded distressed. "Oh no, I think the cotton is about to snap, Niall Orange is being over dramatic announcing that they are all in danger!"

Sharon cried. "I don't think that Niall Orange is being over the top at all, I think all eight of them will need replacing!"

Leon screeched. "The doll has got free, and it's walking around looking for people still singing that it is it's cue to kill everyone!"

Chapter Twenty-Nine

Hovering Dust

Sharon gulped. "Joseph has just appeared, and the doll is walking immediately behind him, I am just thinking, as we have just been discussing accents, I will miss Joseph's Italian accent if he dies as well as Brummie Marie!"

Leon sounded irritated. "The doll is about to breathe on Joseph, but he has lit a match and set the doll on fire!"

Sharon sounded comforted.
"Well, it looks like that is the end of the doll because it is running around like a headless chicken, and I have got an eye joke, the teacher mentioned that they were so bright because they are bright pupils!"

Leon cackled, sounding concerned. "The doll's eye is chasing Joseph around; it's like it is being controlled somehow!"

Sharon took a deep breath. "Joseph has just been attacked by the doll because it's releasing a metal rod out of its eye towards Joseph's stomach!"

Leon sounded at ease. "The metal rod is slowly stabbing Joseph in the stomach. Oh heck, the doll has just collapsed into a heap of ash on the floor with the metal rod collapsing with it!"

Sharon sighed. "I really thought Joseph was following Marie to heaven for a moment then!"

Leon laughed. "It looks like Joseph has had the last laugh on the doll!"

Sharon sounded downhearted. "Sophie Ball has just announced that it's the end of day two of week three with the violins sounding pretty and delicate."

Leon grabbed hold of Sharon's foot. "I will give you a foot massage, you need to relax after that part of the game!"

Sharon sounded hopeful. "Yeah, I do need to take my mind off what has just happened, I just hope that the rest of the players stay alive in the next bit of the game, that was very stressful watching Marie die!"

Leon massaged Sharon's feet. "We could go for a gentle walk, that is, if you would like a walk around where we live!"

Sharon suggested. "Let's walk down this back alley and enjoy each others' bodies in there, I would enjoy that exciting risk of being caught by someone!"

Leon laughed. "Okay, I just hope that it's not a vicar that catches us enjoying each other!"

Sharon laughed. "It definitely won't be children catching us with it being so late, they will definitely see us because of the streetlights above us shining downwards!"

Leon and Sharon dropped their pants with Leon speaking. "This is exciting, I am loving shoving my penis inside of your vagina in full view of the public!"

Sharon took a deep breath. "I am loving this as well. Oh wow, a young-looking male bike rider in his thirties is riding towards us, I guess he is about to ride past us!"

The bike rider shouted as he drove past. "I could do with a bit of that; you look like you are well stuck into each other!"

Leon pushed his penis into Sharon's clit even harder. "You need to find a lady then, because you are not having my lovely Sharon!"

The male bike rider rode off, not looking where he was going riding into a bush shouting. "Oh shucks, ouch, aw that hurt, I am trying to find someone to spend my life with, you look as pretty as a flower Sharon, I will eventually find my special lady that I haven't met as yet unfortunately!"

Sharon laughed. "You will have plenty of sexy nurses to choose from in accident and emergency with you having to go there with you being escorted by some stunning police ladies as well!"

The bike riders' eyes lit up. "Yeah, they will have to patch me up and hopefully give me some extra attention, I may have to have accidents more often because it is a good way to find a sexy lady who can look after me!"

Leon laughed. "I suppose there's always a bright side to a bad situation."

Sharon groaned. "I hope that you find a lady soon, your ambulance is here with some police also wanting to question you as well by the look of it!"

The man on the bike smiled. "I love ladies in uniform; it turns me on even more!"

Leon raised his hand, waving as he was ejaculating. "Well, I think that we have all attracted the attention of everyone in the area, and we are about to be locked up, Sharon!"

Sharon nodded. "The police must be your mates because they are just shaking their heads at us in disbelief!"

Leon chuckled. "Yes, they are my police friends, they have got better things to do than wasting their time arresting us!"

Sharon breathed a sigh of relief. "Thank goodness for that, I was starting to get worried!"

Sharon and Leon walked back to Sharon's house, they went to bed, the next day they went to the park to chill out.

Leon looked at the clock. "I feel so happy because it's that magical time of day, it's pain game time!"

Sharon excitedly jumped. "Yay, Niall Orange has just announced that the beginning of day three of week three is about to start, and the violins are playing calmly!"

Leon squealed. "Oh no, look, the dust on the floor from the doll is swirling around in the air like a swarming cloud, I think the dust is even worse than the freaky doll because it could blow on anyone and kill them!"

Sharon sounded a little stressed. "That dust will probably kill people if it enters people's bodies through their mouths, and the other day, I noticed an advertisement saying that dust is for sale as seen on the television!"

Leon smirked, hesitating to answer. "I feel bad for them all because they have got no chance of staying alive now!"

Sharon struggled for air with sadness in her eyes. "I really don't know if I want to go into the pain game now because I don't want to end my life for a long time yet, so that we can spend plenty more time together, preferably ripping our clothes off and getting hot and steamy in the bedroom!"

Chapter Thirty

Winter Warmer

Leon nodded. "That sounds good to me!"

Sharon glared at the screen. "Ava is walking not far from the hovering dust, she has got three uncooked meat sausages, a Yorkshire pudding shaped in the shape of a cone, gravy, a potato and peas in front of her on a large white plate!"

Leon sounded puzzled. "I wonder what she is supposed to do with the ingredients?"

Sharon sounded surprised. "There is a note at the side of her, it says that Ava needs to make a winter warmer at the same time as random ingredients, and items are being thrown at her at the same time!"

Leon laughed. "How is Ava going to do this with nothing to cook on?"

Sharon sounded puzzled. "I really don't know!"

Leon pointed. "Look, Emma is walking towards Ava, and Ava is explaining what she has got to do to Emma!"

Sharon sounded calm. "I think it's nice of Emma to offer Ava her mirror to make the floor even hotter to cook with, with the sun reflecting on the floor to make it even hotter!"

Leon put his hand up at his mouth in awe. "Emma has just announced that she will come back for the mirror later because half a

Stainless-steel kettle has just missed hitting Ava near her hand!"

Sharon sounded informative. "Niall Orange is talking about how Ava is using half the kettle to cook the sausage in!"

Leon sounded frightened. "Ava is having to duck a lot while she is cooking because there are plastic ducks that are about to hit her on the back of her head!"

Sharon gasped. "It's a good job she isn't looking behind her so that she doesn't get poked in her eyes, and I like the way she is using a duck to mash the potato in the metal stainless-steel bucket that was thrown at her, I find it rather funny, it sounds like Sophie Ball finds it hilarious because she and Niall Orange are finding it hard to talk with them laughing!"

Leon laughed. "At least we are all enjoying the game, I like the way she is using the teapot that was thrown at her to make the gravy!"

Sharon smiled. "I think that Ava is very creative!"

Leon nodded. "Yeah, she is using what tools she has got available to her, she is on the ball!"

Sharon smiled. "At least Ava has finished making the winter warmer, she has perched it inside of the open-lidded teapot!"

Leon glowed. "Yeah, she looks so proud with the mashed potatoes at the base of the Yorkshire pudding with the sausages sticking out of the top like a flake with peas as sprinkles and gravy as sauce, I could eat that myself, it looks so good!"

Sharon licked her lips. "Me too, I have got a feeling that everyone will be making winter warmers at home now, it will be the new trend!"

Leon gasped. "Emma is back with her lovely broad Yorkshire accent, and they are kissing heavily and stripping each others clothes off, I think they still like each other because they are getting into Ava's pop-up tent again for a bit of privacy!"

Sharon's eyes lit up. "Ava has got a note outside of her tent saying that she can enter the safe room for the night, and my guess is that Ava will not be teaching Emma any Spanish, I wish Ava could teach me a bit of Spanish!"

Leon sounded positive. "Yes, I agree with you wink, wink, at least Ava isn't entering into the darkroom, or in the bubble being trapped again, she will have a safe, relaxing night with some food and a relaxing comfy bed, it didn't take Ava long to get dressed and pack up her tent, and enter the safe room for the night!"

Sharon sounded contented. "It looks like Emma is enjoying eating Ava's winter warmer because she is getting well stuck in; I don't think we kiss as passionately as Ava and Emma did!"

Leon smiled. "I think that we do, look, Sophie Ball and Niall Orange are focusing on dopey Chinese Amelia walking towards Brandon!"

Sharon's face glowed. "Wow, Brandon and Amelia are cuddling each other, that kiss earlier must have sparked a light that has warmed their hearts!"

Leon sounded shocked. "Brandon and Amelia have started to strip each others' clothes; I think that they are not bothered by the camera!"

Sharon pointed. "Wow, Brandon and Amelia are entering inside of Brandon's tent, this can only mean they want a bit of privacy to enjoy each other!"

Leon smiled. "I can see the shadow silhouette of Brandon's penis entering into Amelia's vagina, they look to be engrossed with each other… this is turning me on!"

Sharon hesitated to speak. "That's beautiful, Amelia's breasts must be so hard with them both feeling erotically fully turned on!"

Leon shouted. "Go for it Brandon, you deserve it, both of you!"

Sharon smiled. "Brandon and Amelia have got dressed; they look red in the face with a radiant expression!"

Leon pointed. "I would have a similar expression if it was myself, Wow, Amelia is walking away towards a white board with words on it like she is in some kind of trance, but it has got missing letters on it for her to guess what the word was!"

Sharon laughed. "That looks a bit strange, and Niall Orange is boasting that he thinks that he knows all of the six letters that are missing!"

Leon laughed. "Sophie Ball is just laughing at Niall Orange; I think the first word must be condom, obviously, because the first two letters are missing!"

Sharon sounded intrigued. "Amelia has written condom as well, but she is wrong because the answer is random!"

Leon smiled. "The second one has got two middle letters missing, and it's obviously fuck!"

Sharon laughed. "Amelia is wrong again for the second time in a row; the answer is a fork!"

Leon smiled. "Word number three has got the second letter in from the left and the second letter in from the right missing, I think that it must be penis!"

Sharon laughed. "You are wrong again; the answer is pants!"

516

Chapter Thirty-One

Doll Dust Chase

Leon sounded smug. "Amelia has got the first correct answer out of three so far, and at least I tried!"

Sharon sounded confused. "Question number four is obviously pussy because the third letter in the letter and the last letter are missing in the word!"

Leon chuckled. "Amelia has got the answer correct; the answer was pulse!"

Sharon smiled. "I wonder if either of us will get question five correct, my guess is sex with the middle letter missing!"

Leon smirked. "Amelia has got three out of five correct so far, the answer was six!"

Sharon's eyes rolled upwards. "The next and last answer number six is obviously boobs with the fourth letter missing from the start of the word, do you think that I am correct?"

Leon shouted. "Ha ha, the answer six was books, not boobs, Amelia has got the answer correct again, so she has got four out of six of the answers correct!"

Sharon pondered. "I wonder what will happen now that Amelia has got most of the answers, correct?"

Leon looked at Amelia strangely. "Niall Orange has announced that Amelia has got to answer an ultimate final question and if she gets word seven correct, she will be immune from the dust affecting her for the rest of the pain game!"

Sharon expressed her opinion. "If we get picked to enter into the game, I hope that we get immunity from the dust somehow!"

Leon responded. "I hope that Sophie Ball and Niall Orange announce soon who is entering into the pain game!"

Sharon sounded tense. "That answer is obviously racy because the last letter is missing, and that will be seven questions asked!"

Leon sounded vocal. "Amelia is correct thank goodness, she said the answer was race, I feel happy for Amelia that she has got immunity from the dust attacking her for the rest of the pain game!"

Sharon held her head high. "I am also pleased for Amelia; she is walking away with a smile on her face!"

Leon shook with fright. "Oh no, look, the dolls dust is chasing Brandon and it's about to enter into his mouth!"

Sharon breathed heavily. "This is making me feel stressed out, oh shucks, the dust has entered into Brandon's nose, that's Marie and Brandon dead now!"

Leon wiped a tear from his eye. "Yes, you are sadly correct Sharon because Brandon has just fallen to the ground with a bang, and he looks unconscious because he isn't moving a muscle, I will miss Brandon's Scottish accent!"

Sharon sounded worked up. "Amelia will miss Brandon even more than us, and look, the dolls dust has left Brandon's body through his ear, it is like the dust is searching for its next victim!"

Leon sounded gloomy. "It looks like the dust is on a mission to kill them all!"

Sharon sounded downhearted. "Flying Drew has run over to see if

Brandon is alive, I don't think that he is breathing because Drew has got tears in his eyes, and he has just shut Brandon's open unresponsive dead eyes, he looks so down!"

Leon stared at Drew's fingers. "Look, I think that Drew has got a bit of frostbite from the avalanche on his fingers because they look a bit of a blue and white colour with them shaking slightly, I bet his fingers are painful!"

Sharon nodded. "Yes, I think that you are spot on with your opinion,

Drew has gone to wash his hands in the shallow lake bottom, and he is getting some water in his pan at the same time!"

Leon sounded curious. "I bet Drew is just sterilising some water for him to drink, maybe!"

Sharon guessed. "Maybe, or Drew is going to do some cooking with the apples that Ava threw at Amelia that Drew has got in his transparent rook sack that he must have found!"

Leon grinned like a Cheshire Cat. "Yeah, you are correct, Drew is having stewed apples, I bet they will be nice!"

Sharon announced. "Yes, they will be sweet, and as gorgeous as you, I am sure, Niall Orange is announcing that it's the end of day three of week three, I can't believe how fast this game is disappearing beneath my fingers like sand passing through your fingers, in my opinion it should be on for longer!"

Leon moaned. "I know, all of the best things in life don't last long enough, and the violins are playing calmly, and I wonder when someone will find the gold clock?"

Sharon smiled. "Maybe never at this rate, and we will hopefully be together for a long time!"

Leon put his arm around Sharon. "We are a team, me and you; I just want to look after you forever!"

Sharon stroked Leon's face gently. "I love cuddling you, you are the best person in the world!"

Leon picked Sharon up and carried her upstairs. "I will strip you, then I will stroke your body gently; you deserve to be treated like royalty!"

Sharon groaned. "I love it when you touch me, it turns me on so much, and I love stripping you as well!"

Leon could not stop kissing Sharon. "Your lips are so warm and soft, Sharon; they feel like the best thing in the world!"

Sharon cuddled Leon. "You are so sweet; I think your cuddles are the best, Leon!"

Leon stroked Sharon's breast. "Your body is so soft, warm and beautiful Sharon, and your eyes shine brightly, just like diamonds!"

Sharon sighed. "I love it when we are together, you make my world so much better!"

Leon rubbed his penis up and down Sharon's breast. "You are

making me feel so horny, and I feel like ejaculating all over you!"

Sharon smiled. "Please enter your penis inside of my clit, and we can both reach our climax together!"

Chapter Thirty-Two

Safe Room

Leon immediately put his penis inside of Sharon's clit. "I am loving moving in and out of your deep, cosy hole, it feels amazing!"

Sharon gasped. "I love you moving in and out of me, it feels better than eating candy!"

Leon sounded erotic. "I am about to ejaculate inside of you!"

Sharon screamed. "Ooh, yes, please, I can't wait to feel your warm sperm shoot inside of me!"

Leon sounded serious. "Here it comes, my love juices will flow well deep inside of your amazing deep, dark black tight, and soft warm welcoming hole!"

Sharon sighed. "That was lovely, let's go to bed, then we can go to the local music class around the corner, and then we can find out what musical instruments we can learn to play!"

Leon's eyes lit up. "Yes, music class sounds really good to me!"

Sharon and Leon attended music class and then enjoyed food in the Crumbs sandwich shop.

Sharon played her violin that she had borrowed from music class speaking. "I am sure that I will be as good at playing the violin as they are that play at the beginning and end of the pain game if I keep practising!"

Leon laughed. "If you get good enough at playing, maybe you could ask to play at the beginning, and at the end of the last episode of the pain game!"

Sharon nodded. "Maybe, you never know!"

Leon sat on the sofa. "Look, it's the beginning of day four of week three already!"

Sharon looked at a poster dangling down from a tree. "It says that the basilisk's are known as Jesus

Christ Lizards because of their ability to run across the water!"

Leon sounded interested. "These posters are very resourceful!"

Sharon sounded upset. "I agree, look, Amelia is knelt down crying looking at Brandon, I think that Amelia will really miss Brandon because they enjoyed each others' bodies!"

Leon sounded distraught. "Brandon has been through so much with his last moments being his worst nightmare, I bet it was awful when he was stuck inside of the bubble!"

Sharon put her hand on her forehead. "I would have been frightened as well!"

Leon sounded distraught. "This isn't a good situation at all, and I didn't realise how stained Brandon was from being stuck under the strawberries!"

Sharon sounded vocal. "Orr look, Marie and Brandon have been connected to strong strings, and they are getting lifted off the ground into the air by a helicopter with their deceased bodies dangling down … I have no words, only tears!"

Leon sounded shocked. "I am a little surprised that Marie and Brandon's transparent rook sacks have been left behind, containing all of their items on the ground!"

Sharon sounded weepy. "I am not surprised at all because anything that they use will not protect them from the dolls dust killing them!"

Leon wiped a tear from his eye. "Sophie Ball and Niall Orange are announcing that Marie, and Brandon are being taken away to their families so that they can say goodbye to them properly!"

Sharon sounded heartbroken. "Amelia is blowing kisses up to Brandon's body, I have got a lump in my throat, this is heart-wrenching!"

Leon focused on Marie. "Sophie Ball is crying, and Niall Orange is taking over mentioning about Marie's strawberry fingers, with them being stained slightly red!"

Sharon wept. "Yes, it's a sign that she has lived her life, and if she had not have entered the pain game, she would still be alive and kicking with her heart beating out of her chest, instead of her life ending with her having no more of her life to live!"!"

Leon sounded a little sad. "There are only six contestants left playing now, I wonder who will lose their lives next?"

Sharon nodded. "At least there are less of them to win the jackpot, and I am sure that more people will enter into the game soon to join Amelia, Benjamin, Joseph, Ava, Drew, and Emma!"

Leon sounded shocked. "There is a board saying that two people need to play a card game called snap, and the winner will win a night away in the safe room like Emma did!"

Sharon was in deep thought. "Well, Amelia may as well keep away from the game because she has got immunity from the dust already!"

Leon agreed. "That is so true, I wonder which of them will turn up!"

Sharon highlighted her view. "Joseph has just appeared with his pan full of water that he was slowly drinking!"

Leon was taken aback. "Drew has appeared, he doesn't look very happy though because he must be fed up, and in pain!"

Sharon watched Drew and Joseph closely. "Neither of them looks overly cheerful, and Joseph has still got blood on his clothes from cauterising Benjamin's bottom!"

Leon looked interested. "I suppose they are experiencing something that we will hopefully never have to experience!"

Sharon sounded anxious. "The dust is hovering near to Drew and Joseph; whoever wins, I guess the dust will kill the unlucky victim!"

Leon gasped. "Sophie Ball has just mentioned that the one with the most cards at the end of the game with the cards that they have matched wins!"

Sharon crossed her fingers. "I wish them all the luck in the world!"

Leon sounded saddened. "This is so tense; they have started to play, and the stack of cards looks so small, so it will not take very long for either Joseph or Drew to win the night in the safe room or be choked to death by some doll dust!"

Sharon guessed. "I wonder who will win the game and the jackpot?"

Chapter Thirty-Three

Viewing Shed

Leon sounded stressed. "We will find out soon because Drew and Joseph have started to play snap!"

Five minutes ticked by with Sharon sounding tense. "This game is getting nerve-racking, because Drew has obviously won more cards than Joseph, I think Joseph will be the next dead dust victim!"

Leon shook his head in disbelief. "Joseph has thrown his cards into the air in a rage, and Niall Orange has just announced that Drew has won the game of snap!"

Sharon screamed. "Oh no, look, the doll dust is about to attack Joseph!"

Leon sounded horrified. "The doll dust is about to enter inside of Joseph's mouth!"

Sharon sounded flabbergasted. "Joseph has just thrown his pan of water onto the doll dust, making it all clump together and fall to the ground in a pile!"

Leon sounded surprised. "That was lucky that Joseph had his pan of water at the side of him, he just needs to keep throwing water at the dust to keep alive until the end of the pain game!"

Sharon sounded a little happier. "At least on the upside, Drew will enjoy a relaxing night in the safe room!"

Leon agreed. "Yes, that sounds good to me, Joseph will have to keep his pan full of water ready to throw at the dust, and do you know what you call a dusty skeleton?"

Sharon quizzed. "I don't know!"

Leon answered. "The grimy reaper!"

Sharon laughed, stating. "It looks like Joseph's mouth is still in pain from his abscess or whatever he had wrong with him before he entered into the jungle with the needle enhancing, inflicting every pain that he has ever had!"

Leon moaned. "Niall Orange and Sophie Ball are announcing the end of day four of week three and the violins sound great!"

Sharon sounded disappointed. "We need to go up to bed and massage each other to cheer ourselves up!"

Leon nodded. "Yes, I think a cuddle is the best medicine to cheer us up!"

Sharon sounded relaxed. "This is really soothing; your hands feel so soft on my back!"

Leon put some baby oil on Sharon's back. "I am just glad that you are relaxed, Sharon!"

Sharon muttered. "I am so calm and relaxed that I am falling asleep!"

Leon whispered to Sharon, giving her a gentle kiss on her cheek. "You go to sleep, my love, and we can chat in the morning!"

The next morning Leon made Sharon a coffee and a bacon sandwich in bed, they then went for a walk around Pugneys Country Park with Sharon speaking. "Let's go into the bird viewing shed and enjoy looking at the birds!"

Leon started to kiss Sharon. "It would be exciting to play with each other in here!"

Sharon's eyes lit up. "Yeah, that would be fun, I just hope nobody comes in to view some birds!"

Leon smiled. "I am viewing my bird right here and now!"

Sharon sounded up-spirited. "I have got my perfect bird and there is nobody around, please fill my clit with your penis!"

Sharon removed her trousers with Leon speaking. "I am loving touching and feeling every part of you and filling your clit!"

Sharon could not stop kissing Leon speaking. "I can hear footsteps outside of the bird viewing shed!"

Leon sounded panicked. "Oh heck, that means that we will not be alone in a second!"

Sharon did not sound bothered. "They can come in if they like, I don't care right now!"

Leon chuckled. "I am about to spurt up inside of your clit!"

A younger lady walked into the shed, speaking. "It looks like you have both had fun birdwatching in a more exciting and unpredictable fun way!"

Sharon smirked. "Oh yeah, we have had lots of fun, if you had come in a minute earlier, you would have seen us birdwatching for real in an outrageous manner that you can only imagine!"

Leon and Sharon enjoyed food at the Crumbs sandwich shop on their way home, they then relaxed on the sofa having a cuddle.

Leon announced. "It's that time of day again with the violins playing, Sophie Ball has announced the beginning of day five of week three!"

Sharon sounded giddy. "Niall Orange has publicised that they have picked a person to enter into the pain game as a new player from the home viewers, I feel so excited, do you think that we will be in with a chance of entering into the Central American jungle?"

Leon sounded intrigued. "Niall Orange mentioned that one person had been picked so maybe one of us could enter!"

Sharon sounded hopeful. "I do hope so, I wonder when we will find out if we will have the chance of winning the jackpot!"

Leon sounded a little negative. "Don't get your hopes up because we will probably be disappointed with our dreams hitting the floor with a bang and smashing into a million little pieces, scattering everywhere!"

Sharon was not put off by what Leon had said, still sounding ecstatic. "If we win a place in the pain game, it will be a one-in-a-lifetime opportunity for us to get a go at changing our lives for the better!"

Leon sounded a little bit disappointed. "Sophie Ball has just announced that we have got to wait until the end of tonights game to find out who has won a place in the jungle!"

Sharon sounded a little surprised. "Niall Orange has just reported that the person that wins will be live on webcam in a private plane tomorrow night with him or her enjoying a relaxing massage, and there will be a comfy bed for them to relax on until they get parachuted into the jungle from the private plane!"

Leon pointed. "There is a small blue car in the jungle, and there is a note saying car ram at the side of it on a note on a piece of paper!"

Chapter Thirty-Four

Yellow

Sharon looked oddly at many different sized boxes at the side of the car. "It says that someone needs to fit every box into the car boot within five minutes!"

Leon gasped. "I dread to think what will happen if the person that does the challenge loses!"

Sharon raised her eyebrows at Emma walking towards the car." Oh no, Emma is in double trouble now because she is trying to run away with no success, and she is running on the spot!"

Leon pulled a frightened face with him biting his lips. "That's Emma, maybe the next to lose her life!"

Sharon sounded upset. "A timer of five minutes is on the car number plate with it counting down slowly!"

Leon had a look of dread in his eyes. "Emma has started putting boxes into the car already, and she is already juggling them around to make sure that they fit with not even a minute gone by yet!"

Sharon sounded uneasy. "I am worried about Emma; she will probably not finish the challenge!"

Leon screamed. "Two minutes have gone by already and Emma has removed more boxes than she has put in the boot!"

Sharon sounded stressed. "Three minutes have ticked by now, and Emma is still nowhere near filling the car boot!"

Leon breathed heavily. "Four minutes have gone by now, and there's still no sign of the car boot being full!"

Sharon sounded on edge. "Emma is trying her hardest to make all of the boxes fit into the car boot with the last-minute ticking away even faster!"

Leon gritted his teeth. "Well, it looks like Emma has filled the boot just in time with a second left to spare!"

Sharon pointed. "Look, Drew is leaving the safe room, and Emma is walking towards the safe room!"

Leon smiled. "I am happy that Emma has been rewarded with a night in the safe room, it will feel like she is in a five-star luxury hotel!"

Sharon pointed. "Drew is at risk of being killed now!"

Leon sounded unfazed. "I hope that Drew will be okay, but this game is unpredictable, and we have found out that we can't change what is going to happen!"

Sharon sounded in shock. "Niall Orange has mentioned that Marie's mother Jane is sitting in the private plane waiting to set off on her journey to the jungle, she looks a little teary!"

Leon shed a tear. "She is going to the last place that her daughter stood, I am not surprised that she is upset!"

Sharon's ears pricked open. "Listen, Jane is announcing that she is going to try to win the money jackpot for Marie that she could have won if she were still alive!"

Leon sounded unsurprised. "That doesn't surprise me at all, Jane needs to do something to make her daughters death mean something, I suppose!"

Sharon sounded gooey. "That's nice, she sounds exactly like Marie with her Brummie accent, and I am glad that Jane enjoyed her massage before her stress begins!"

Leon sounded distracted. "My neighbour is obviously putting her rubbish in the outside bin, that sounded so loud!"

Sharon suggested. "Let's send a piece of rubbish into the pain game that may be of some use in the jungle!"

Leon's eyes lit up. "This large yellow plastic shopping bag that I used this morning, I will donate this, I have got the address that I need to send it to on the pain games website!"

Sharon laughed. "I don't know what they would do with a yellow shopping bag, but I am sure it will not go to waste!"

Leon smiled. "We can send the shopping bag first thing in the morning first class!"

Sharon smirked. "We can't enter into the pain game, but Niall Orange has just announced that we can enter to go live from our home in the jungle on week six!"

Leon glanced at Sharon's hand, grabbing hold of it. "Wow, that will be exciting if we can listen to the players reactions to us live on webcam, I really do think that it is just a shame that we will not win any money!"

Sharon giggled. "Yeah, we can enter to go live on webcam from home now while we are watching!"

Leon sounded surprised. "Sophie Ball has just mentioned that we can say whatever we want live on the webcam to the whole entire nation watching the pain game!"

Sharon sounded unsure. "That's if we win, Sophie Ball will possibly regret saying that we can say what we like if we win the opportunity to go live, and yes, it is a shame we will not win any money!"

Leon sounded hopeful. "We have entered our chance to go into the pain game; all we can do now is see what happens!"

Sharon sounded disappointed. "Sophie Ball is announcing that it's the end of day five of week three, and the violins sound dramatic!"

Leon walked over to a vibrator. "I got this so that you can have my penis in your anus, and the vibrator in your clit at the same time if you like?"

Sharon nodded. "Yes, let's do it, it will be fun!"

Leon laughed. "I am just thinking about my friend, he met a girl with her little brother having bunk beds, so he said that they were making sandwiches in bed!"

Sharon chuckled. "What happened?"

Leon explained. "Well, in their secret code, cheese meant thrust in harder and tomato meant faster!"

Sharon gasped. "Did the little boy really know what was going on?"

Leon broke into hysterics. "The little boy screamed for them to stop making sandwiches in bed because mayonnaise was spraying all over his bed!"

Sharon smirked. "You are funny and daft, come on then, fill both of my holes, I am getting turned on thinking about it!"

Leon pushed the dildo into Sharon's clit in between, filling her anus with his penis. "This is fun Sharon!"

Sharon sighed. "I know I am loving it; you concentrate on pushing into my anus while I control my clit if you like for another few minutes!"

Leon sounded erotic. "I am really enjoying filling you; I will be spurting my own mayonnaise in a minute into your anus!"

Sharon was screaming with pleasure. "This is amazing, we should do this again!"

Leon pushed into Sharon's anus harder. "I think that we are both getting more than a fun buzz out of this!"

Sharon pulled the dildo out of her clit. "Please move into my clit and fill me with your amazing sperm!"

Chapter Thirty-Five

Clock

Leon moved into Sharon's clit with his penis. "I can't hold it back anymore; I am at my climax ejaculating inside of you!"

Sharon just laid down, enjoying every drop of Leon's creamy love juices. "I needed that! "

Leon suggested going to bed then going to the sunbed shop and they can then enjoy touching each other while they tan, and then go to the Crumbs sandwich shop, and then for a massage at West Yorkshire Massage.

Sharon and Leon relaxed when they got back to Sharon's house with Leon announcing. "The violins are playing an upbeat tune, and Niall Orange is introducing the beginning of day six of week three!"

Sharon sounded relaxed. "That sun bed was warm, it made me feel like I was in the jungle for a minute!"

Leon sounded uneasy. "Sophie Ball has just announced that Jane will be entering into the jungle tomorrow night with a chance of winning the jackpot, I hope that she finds the clock!"

Sharon sounded hopeful. "Me too, and I hope that Jane wins the money, she deserves a bit of good luck with her daughter Marie losing her life!"

Leon sounded worried. "That pain-enhancing needle will not help Jane because she will be in agony!"

Sharon agreed. "At least Amelia, Benjamin, Joseph, Ava, Drew and Emma will have the advantage of their pain wearing off a little with nearly three weeks gone by with it improving a little bit for them by now, or they will have got used to the pain, maybe!"

Leon pulled a face by pulling his jaw downwards slightly. "I am glad that we don't have to have the pain-enhancing needle like Jane!"

Sharon wiped a tear from her eye. "Marie and Brandon didn't even get a sniff of the money, I think that's so sad going through all of that danger with nothing to show for it with no reward at the end, just death and never to be seen again!"

Leon pointed. "At least the pain game will keep them alive in people's memories and look, Dopey Amelia is walking towards a poster saying Hannah says, I wonder what that's all about?"

Sharon read the writing, with it appearing as if it was freshly written on a poster. "You only have to do it when it says Hannah says to do it!"

Leon sounded a little puzzled. "It looks like Amelia is in a trance because she has got a bland expression on her face!"

Sharon gulped. "Below the poster, it says find the doll dust and eat it!"

Leon sounded tense. "With my understanding of what the poster says,

Amelia doesn't have to do that because it doesn't say What Hannah says!"

Sharon took a deep breath. "Amelia is about to walk around; she hasn't read what it says properly at all on the poster!"

Leon breathed heavily, panting a little. "The dust is just there, and she is opening her mouth, looking and sounding exhausted!"

Sharon sounded upset. "Drew has just tried to drag Amelia away from the doll dust, but it has followed Amelia and it's about to enter into her nose!"

Leon laughed. "The doll dust has ejected from Amelia's breath as she breathes because she has got immunity from the dust from killing her!"

Sharon smiled. "That's good, I forgot that Dopey Chinese Amelia has got immunity from the dust for a minute!"

Leon sounded intrigued. "A bell has just rung, and some more writing has appeared saying Hannah says dance around!"

Sharon gasped. "Thew, I thought Amelia was a goner then as well, it is a good job that flying Drew turned up to save Amelia even though he didn't really need to!"

Leon sounded appalled. "The dust is trying to enter inside of Drew's mouth now, but he has trapped the doll dust inside of his hot water bottle by putting the lid on, and Drew is throwing his hot water bottle onto the floor in a rage, and he has walked away from Amelia!"

Sharon smiled. "It's nice to see Amelia dancing, she looks a little jolly because she's got a slight smile on her face, I guess that she is smiling because the dust is trapped inside of Drew's hot water bottle!"

Leon's eyes followed Amelia around. "The bell has rung again, and it says climb a tree!"

Sharon sounded relieved. "At least Amelia is ignoring what it says, and she is standing on the spot!"

Leon agreed. "At least Amelia is getting the hang of the game a bit!"

Sharon's eyes turned towards Leon's eyes, with her rolling her eyes. "This is silly, it now says, Hannah says if you can catch a fish from the lake bottom within two minutes using her fishing rod, she will win!"

Leon sounded sad. "Amelia has got no chance of catching a fish in two minutes!"

Sharon sounded thunderstruck. "Oh no, Amelia has lost, and she is walking towards the bubble that Ava was stuck inside of!"

Amelia was crying as she walked into the bubble. "The heat is making me feel dehydrated and it feels claustrophobic already!"

Leon looked at the bright side. "At least Ava could use her orange button to release herself from the bubble!"

Sharon sounded baffled. "I don't know how Amelia will get out?"

Leon sounded positive. "Emma has just walked past because she is out of the safe room now!"

Sharon watched something drop from a drone in the sky. "How strange, a box of straws has just fallen from the drone!"

Leon laughed. "It must be a useless item that someone watching the pain game has sent in for the contestants to use, the drone has gone from sight now!"

Sharon lifted both sides of her lips, forcing a smile. "Look, Emma is picking a straw out of the packet!"

Leon guessed. "Emma will probably keep the straw as a tool in case she needs it later!"

Chapter Thirty-Six

Maze Walls

Sharon pointed, "I think you are spot on, look. Joseph is staring at Amelia crying stuck inside of the bubble!"

Leon sounded sad. "I think that Joseph must feel helpless because he cannot help Amelia!"

Sharon stared at Joseph. "A large maze has appeared in front of Joseph and Niall Orange is being over dramatic with how large it is!"

Leon looked at the maze strangely. "I think that is a really odd thing to see in the jungle!"

Sharon stared at the top of the walls of the green plant maze. "It's really odd to see ruffled grouse birds resting on every spare inch available!"

Leon sounded puzzled." It is like the ruffled grouse birds are ganging up to attack someone and Sophie Ball is saying the same as me!"

Sharon agreed. "There is a small bag full of green grapes in the entrance of the maze, what an odd thing to see!"

Leon stared at Joseph, picking the bag up and eating the green grapes. "It's like the grapes are turning Joseph into a drunk state because he's falling all over the place!"

Sharon laughed. "Joseph is bouncing off all of the hedge walls, and it says on the hedge written in flowers that he has got a day to find the exit, or he will be sent into the darkroom!"

Leon sounded concerned. "Niall Orange is mentioning that there must be alcohol injected into the grapes, as Joseph finishes or has had enough of the grapes, he will be sober again!"

Sharon nodded. "It certainly looks like Joseph has had a few too many!"

Leon sounded shocked. "Joseph is talking to the hedge; I think he has lost the plot!"

Sharon sniggers. "I personally think that Joseph must be hallucinating, or he is very drunk!"

Leon demanded. "Joseph needs to get out of the maze sooner rather than later or he could die of thirst in the darkroom!"

Sharon sounded devastated. "Oh no, Niall Orange is announcing that it's the end of day six of week three and the violins are being played so nicely!"

Leon sounded disappointed. "We will have to wait until tomorrow's game to find out what happens to Joseph!"

Sharon tried to cheer Leon up. "I am trying to lift your mood, please stop being miserable, we will find out what happens tomorrow to Joseph!"

Leon smiled. "Okay, you are right, it's only a game at the end of the day, I suppose after all!"

Sharon tickled Leon's head. "How does that feel, is it nice?"

Leon shut his eyes. "Wow, yes, that feels like a proper head massage, that's so relaxing Sharon!"

Sharon moved downwards to Leon's shoulder. "I want to massage your whole body; you need to completely destress yourself, Leon!"

Leon made ooh noises. "That's so nice, I could sit here all day while you massage me!"

Sharon kissed Leon on his lips. "We can massage each other's lips for a bit, Leon!"

Leon licked downwards, unbuttoning Sharon's top. "Your breasts are so firm, and they feel as soft as a babies bottom, Sharon!"

Sharon sounded relaxed. "You are like a breath of fresh air, Leon, and you always smell nice!"

Leon and Sharon stripped each other while Leon was speaking. "I will lick you moving down to your smooth shaven, clean, lovely smiling clit!"

Sharon groaned. "Your tongue turns me on so much, and when you talk, doing anything to me makes me feel so hot and steamy under the collar!"

Leon sounded excited. "I can tell that I turn you on because you are so wet, I am going to lick your clit and then fill you with my penis!"

Sharon smiled. "I love it when you are so assertive, it turns me on even more!"

Leon spoke in between licking Sharon's clit. "This is making me feel so randy, I am moving in with my penis!"

Sharon wiped the sweat from her eyebrow. "This feels so intensely amazing with every thrust that you make!"

Leon expressed his feelings. "This is so special and pleasurable; I love us being close to each other's warm, and delicate skin, you satisfy my every need!"

Sharon groaned. "You are so precious to me; I wouldn't ever want anybody else!"

Leon softly spoke. "I am going to reward you with my warm sperm!"

Sharon sounded outspoken. "Oh yeah, go for it!"

Leon sounded relieved. "I have filled your lovely vagina with my love seeds!"

Sharon smiled. "I feel full filled now, let's go to Sandal Castle tomorrow for a walk around, and then play chess until the pain game starts!"

Leon nodded. "That sounds good to me, let's go to bed, and then we can enjoy ourselves tomorrow, we need to make the most of the time that we have got left before we have got to go back to work!"

Sharon and Leon enjoyed the next day; the end of the day arrived with Sharon speaking. "Wow, it's that time of the day again!"

Leon sounded ecstatic. "I am loving listening to the violins; they sound so full of joy; I hope that you can play live on the pain game one day before the game show ends!"

Sharon agreed. "Me too, look, it's the start of day seven of week three!"

Leon pointed. "Look, Joseph is still looking like he is a bit lost and dazed in the maze, it's a bit different than bubbles!"

Sharon gasped. "Niall Orange is announcing that Joseph's time is nearly up in the maze, and people have got to replace whoever loses until someone makes it to the end!"

Chapter Thirty-Seven

Darkroom

Leon stared at the poster that the camera was focusing on. "What an awesome photo of a hummingbird, and it says below the photo that it is almost impossible to click a picture of it because they fly away so fast!"

Sharon pondered. "Yes, I suppose most birds do fly away fast, and yes, it is a shame that not many people can get photos of the hummingbird!"

Leon sounded comforted. "That is lovely, and I think I would rather be here having a better way of life with you, I feel sorry for the players' with their lives hanging in the balance of life-or-death situations!"

Sharon agreed. "Me too, at least we have got each other to help each other through any bad times!"

Leon caught his breath. "Sophie Ball is welcoming Marie's mother Jane into the jungle, she will find it really hard with the brutal horrendous, difficult tasks, and conditions, and her age could go against her with her being older than the others because she will not be able to move or think as fast on her feet!"

Sharon struggled for breath. "That pain-enhancing needle looks scary, I bet Jane will be in so much pain when she has that injected inside of her, and it will be strange for Jane to stand where Marie last stood, I guess that it will be a nightmare or a comfort!"

Leon sounded a little curiously puzzled. "I wonder how

they invented something so horrible that causes every pain to come back all at once throughout your entire life that you have ever lived!"

Sharon sounded a little sad. "I don't know, but Jane will find out with how much pain she will be experiencing in a second as soon as that needle leaves her arm!"

Leon stared at Jane. "Jane is holding her head in her hands;

she must have had some sort of a bad head injury at some point in her life for her to behave like that!"

Sharon sounded hopeful. "I wish her luck, but I think her chances of winning are low!"

Leon sounded interested. "Jane has got a sun hat, a gun, tarpaulin, a small knife, a fishing rod, and a pan included in her six items!"

Sharon blew outwards. "Wow, Jane has got a gun, this could get messy with more lives lost!"

Leon wiped a tear from his eye. "Jane has walked off; she looks like she is really struggling with her pain in her head!"

Sharon sounded a little shocked. "I think that Joseph has got no chance of finding the finish line because the drone is showing that Joseph is bang in the middle of the maze, and Sophie Ball thinks that it is funny the way Joseph is shouting at himself in his Italian accent!"

Leon agreed. "I think the same, Joseph will sadly be in the darkroom by the end of today, or this is my guess, I bet he would rather be trying to get rid of the drone again!"

Sharon's eyes nearly popped out of her sockets. "Look, the

ruffled grouse birds are surrounding Joseph, he looks a bit freaked out because he's shaking!"

Leon could not look shielding his eyes with a tiny bit still showing between his fingers. "The grouse birds are flying near to Joseph's face and skimming past him, just missing the top of his head!"

Sharon sounded disturbed. "I would hate the sound of the grouse birds' wings because I would feel so uncomfortable and awkward running away in the opposite direction, the grouse birds are dropping their bowels into Joseph's face, that's totally disgusting, I bet that he wishes that he is falling into some water again!"

Leon nodded. "Yeah, you probably would run in the opposite

direction Sharon, but Joseph has got no choice in the matter and Joseph still looks badly bruised from flying through the air from the darkroom!"

Sharon pointed. "Joseph is getting pecked on the top of his head by many ruffled grouse birds!"

Leon sounded shocked. "Oh no, the birds are drawing blood

because blood is pouring down Joseph's head into his eyes!"

Sharon sounded upset. "I really do think that Joseph must be in shock because he is lying down on the ground shaking badly, and crying, stroking his damaged finger, and massaging his mouth!"

Leon sounded sympathetic. "I am not surprised because Joseph must be in so much pain, I bet he doesn't know what to rub better first between his mouth, finger, nose and generally his whole body!"

Sharon stared at Joseph. "An alligator is chasing Joseph now; it looks so frightening; I think someone will need to help by cauterising him, Joseph was kind, cauterising Marie, and Benjamin, I bet they wish they could focus on a new project, or situation happening that is more positive.

Leon screamed. "As Joseph is attempting to run away from the alligator, the ruffled grouse birds are still chasing him as well as pecking his head!"

Sharon gulped. "This is a very dramatic and dangerous drastic situation for Joseph; Niall Orange is laughing at Joseph because he is blowing his whistle to try to scare the ruffled grouse birds away unsuccessfully!"

Leon sounded upset. "I can't believe this is happening to Joseph; he looks so frightened!"

Sharon stared. "Oh no, look, the alligator is about to eat Joseph's head!"

Leon started playing with his fingers. "Stroking his dart-damaged finger is the last of Joseph's worries!"

Sharon started to cry. "I don't know how Joseph has managed to do it, but he has just hit the alligator over the side of its head with his thick book, it's knocked Joseph's head from its mouth!"

Leon shouted. "Well done, Joseph, I think he needs to run to find the exit, even though the grouse-ruffled birds are still pecking at his head, making his blood spill!

Sharon gazed at Emma, looking at the entrance to the maze. "It's like Emma is in some kind of trance, she is trying to turn and walk away from the maze unsuccessfully!"

Leon observed the situation. "Emma looks so petrified of the maze; and unfortunately for Emma, more ruffled grouse birds are hovering around the entrance!"

Sharon caught her breath. "The ruffled grouse birds have picked Emma up by her clothes, and she has been carried to where Joseph is standing!"

Leon pointed. "There is a note on the hedge written in red roses saying that Joseph is running out of time, and Emma has got until the next day to get out!"

Sharon sounded intrigued. "I do wonder if Joseph will get out alive!"

Leon screeched. "Joseph has wedged his pen in the alligator's mouth, but it's just bitten it and it's now trying to attack Emma!"

Chapter Thirty-Eight

Juicy

Sharon sounded mesmerised. "Emma is using her lipstick knife to kill the alligator, and she is stabbing the birds with it in between!"

Leon sounded concerned. "Emma is using her pan as a weapon now to finish the alligator, and the grouse birds off!"

Sharon sounded shocked. "Emma has grabbed hold of Joseph's hand, and they're running around trying to find the exit!"

Leon shook his head. "I don't think Joseph and Emma will find the exit, but they are trying their best running around to find it!"

Sharon sounded appalled. "The violins are playing a dramatic tune, and Sophie Ball has just announced that they will make Joseph's fait public at the beginning of day one of week four!"

Leon sounded downhearted. "That's disappointing, they like to keep us waiting in the dark to see what will happen next!"

Sharon agreed. "I agree, but it's not right leaving us in the dark with us not knowing what will happen next!"

Leon turned off the television and then started to kiss Sharon on the lips. "Your hair is so soft when I stroke it, you are such a sweet, beautiful, passionate kisser; it feels like I always have butterflies in my stomach when we kiss!"

Sharon nodded. "Yeah, I feel like I am skipping a beat when we are together, we are such a passionate couple, your skin touching mine turns me on even more, I love you to the bones!"

Leon and Sharon cuddled. "I feel like we are a couple of intimate love birds that will never leave each other's side, Sharon!"

Sharon kissed Leon. "I totally agree with you; we are like a couple of penguins or swans that glide along twittering away together sharing our opinions, and daily moans and groans!"

Leon moved downwards, kissing Sharon's breasts. "Your breasts could do with some strawberry juice on them, I noticed some in the cupboard earlier, I will just go and get it!"

Sharon grinned. "I will smell nice and sweet on the upside!"

Leon poured strawberry juice all over Sharon's breast. "Your breasts taste even more juicy than they normally do, and I will hopefully be stuck to you forever!"

Sharon gulped. "You need to lick my clit next, please!"

Leon nodded. "I will do now that I have licked all of the strawberry juice from your body, I will lick you and then fill you like placing apples inside of an apple pie!"

Sharon sounded giddy. "Your tongue feels so warm, and you are completely filling my every need!"

Leon moved his tongue from Sharon's clit, replacing it with his penis. "You feel so tenderly amazing down there!"

Sharon shut her eyes, enjoying every second. "That's amazing the way that you are thrusting inside of my clit, you have got an amazing, unique finger movement making me feel lovely and tingly in a relaxing way!"

Leon announced. "I am ejaculating my warm sperm inside of you any second!"

Sharon groaned. "Please give me every drop!"

Leon smiled and then suggested that they should go to bed. "Now that I have ejaculated, let's go to bed, then tomorrow we can go to the cinema to watch a film!"

The next day, they watched a movie and then relaxed at Sharon's house with Sharon sounding excited.

"Look, it's the start of day one of week four, and the violins sound upbeat!"

Leon pointed. "A lion is walking towards Joseph; it sounds very fierce with it roaring so loudly, I can't believe that something so dangerous can look so cute and soft!"

Sharon sounded beside herself. "Sophie Ball sounds well melodramatic as usual, and the lion's teeth look very sharp like they could easily snap an iron bar like toffee!"

Leon spoke his mind. "I didn't know that a lion's mouth was so large, and I definitely would not want to be in the path of those teeth, they look so dangerous, I would be chewed and shredded up into a million tiny little pieces and never be seen again if it was me!"

Sharon sounded disappointed. "Oh no, Joseph is about to feel how sharp the lion's teeth are because his arm will be gone, then the rest of him will disappear as fast!"

Leon sounded panicked. "Niall Orange is looking at Joseph because the lion is ravaging more than his arm, most of his chest has disappeared now, he's got no chance of survival because he's lost far too much blood and muscle to stay alive and healthy!"

Sharon started to cry. "Oh heck, the lion has got Joseph on the floor, and it's eating him alive!"

Leon pulled a frowning face. "Ewe, that's Joseph not going back home to his family, he will have a foot left to take home to his family, and that's if he is lucky for them to morn over!"

Sharon bawled her eyes out. "I really can't deal with this game, it's a bit too gory, sad, and bloody disgusting sometimes!"

Leon wiped a tear away. "I feel sorry for Joseph's family; they will have nothing left to berry so they can put their minds at rest that they have given him a good send-off!"

Sharon shrieked. "Emma looks totally devastated; she is crying uncontrollably on the floor staring at Joseph's lifeless, deceased body!"

Leon nodded. "Yeah, I feel really sorry for Emma because the lions are about to go for her, she needs to run away now fast!"

Sharon sounded distraught. "Well, that's Marie, Joseph, and Brandon who are dead now!"

Leon struggled to speak with crying. "Yes, and Joseph's family may have nothing left to berry that's the saddest part!"

Sharon picked up the television remote control. "I feel like turning it off, but I can't because I need to know what will happen to Emma!"

Leon sat opened mouthed in awe. "Jane has appeared, Sophie Ball sounds shocked that Jane is standing next to Emma, heavily smashing the lion on its head with her pan and stabbing it!"

Please read Book Two for more drama.

About the author

Anita Kirk is from Yorkshire in the United Kingdom, she works full time and writes many book genres in her spare time with unlimited talent to write anything, she loves swimming, line dancing, holidays, music, films, writing, reading and spending time with friends and family.

All of Anita Kirk's books have got <u>funny moments</u> that may make you feel like laughing your socks off.

In a Quarter of a second and the Glowing Rings has got two magical action-packed time travel adventures inside.

Dream Changing is about a lady who can see people's dreams and can change them.
Does Flora help to save the world after visiting the opticians receiving more hassle and drama than she bargained for?

Sexy Antics is for adults to enjoy; you will never look at a magazine in the same way again.

Magical Footsteps has got a friend that has gone missing that needs finding with help from strangers, with them ending up inside of a game.

Unexpected Jewel has got different stories inside full of mythical creatures, and it is full of magic.

Sexy Shenanigans has got four stories for adults to enjoy with the last story having horror inside as well.

Christmas Sparkles has got fairies inside of this book and a fairytale cottage where they live, the fairies need help from two children and other people to get people onto the nice list to save Christmas, with so much more inside for you to enjoy.

Mel's Adventure has got a story with pictures for the younger end or anyone that needs a simple story to learn the alphabet, with a song and a few words in a different language to learn as well.

The Sound of Ticking is about a man who owns a shop in New York and receives a telescope for his birthday, his life is soon turned upside down with unpredictable challenging situations taking him to many places in time to solve many mysteries.

Wings to Heaven. This is a true story about my dad's life before,

during and after dementia and Alzheimer's.

TIME TRAVEL LIP BALM
Enjoy the adventure, the lip balm dramas inside of this book are very unpredictable and fun, it's full of jokes and lighthearted entertainment for anyone to enjoy from adults to children.

Sexy Revenge is for adults only, it's about a man that has a car accident, and his life is stolen by his best friend while he's in a coma, does Jenson kick some ass getting his own back?

Fun Dance Book One has got many dances to follow by yourself or with others, it is ideal for any age.

Spooky Scary needs garlic circles and so much more to bring people back to normal everyday life with many obstacles and drama along the way.

These books have been written so far with many more available soon.

Remember that you can follow and contact Anita Kirk with any questions or comments on Tick Tock, Facebook, Twitter, LinkedIn or you can email any comments to
anitajane1@outlook.com
Please contact Anita if you would like a shop opening or anything else and she will get back to you as soon as possible with an answer.
If you have enjoyed reading Anita Kirk's books a good review would be appreciated and if you could share Anita's books on your social media, and with your family and friends she would really appreciate your help.

Thank you for your support in
reading this book.
All of Anita Kirk's books are
available on Amazon and
some other online shops.

Thank you again

PLEASE·TYPE·ANITA·KIRK·INTO·AMAZON¶

FOR·ALL·AVAILABLE·PUBLISHED·BOOKS¶

OF·MANY·DIFFERENT·GENRES.·¶

__Erotically Spooky__ is the __same__ as __Spooky Scary__ but it has got a little bit of raunch, and vampires attempt to take over the world with funny moments to make you laugh out loud.

__Thank you.__

Anita Kirk, author
@AnitaKi73550337

Twitter –

Author Anita Kirk

LinkedIn-

Instagram-

__Please don't forget to leave a good review if you have enjoyed reading this book and share it with others on social media or in person.__

__Thank you again.__

<u>You can also follow Anita Kirk on</u>

@anitakirkauthor ▣

<u>*tick tock.*</u>

www.ingramcontent.com/pod-product-compliance
Lightning Source LLC
Chambersburg PA
CBHW072345030726
47505CB00015B/1928